RISE
OF THE
GUARDIANS

RISE
OF THE
GUARDIANS

MOVIE NOVELIZATION

adapted by Stacia Deutsch

SIMON AND SCHUSTER

This book is a work of fiction. Any references to historical events, real people, or real places are used fictitiously. Other names, characters, places, and events are products of the author's imagination, and any resemblance to actual events or places or persons, living or dead, is entirely coincidental.

Simon and Schuster
First published in Great Britain in 2012 by Simon & Schuster UK Ltd
1st Floor, 222 Gray's Inn Road, London WC1X 8HB
A CBS Company
Published in the USA in 2012 by Simon Spotlight, an imprint of
Simon & Schuster Children's Division, New York.

10 9 8 7 6 5 4 3 2 1
A CIP catalogue record for this book is available from the British Library
ISBN   978-1-4711-1631-5
Printed and bound in Slovakia by TBB, a. s.

CHAPTER
ONE

Long ago, the surface of a frozen pond cracked when Jack Frost rose out of the icy water. He was thin, pale, and barefoot. His white hair glistened as he looked around. Nothing was familiar. Not even his reflection.

"But then I saw the moon. It was so big and it was so bright, and it seemed to chase the darkness away. And when it did . . , I wasn't scared anymore," he remembered.

Jack walked across the ice-covered Pond until he hit something with his foot. He reached down to pick up a wooden staff. Almost immediately the staff began to glow a bright blue.

It was so strange, Jack nearly dropped it. As the base of the staff came in contact with the ground, frost shot out and spread across the ice.

Jack shook his head. He didn't know what was happening.

Experimenting, he touched the staff to a tree. It sent a stream of frost up the trunk.

The staff was magical. Jack discovered he could command the wind to carry him up into the trees. From a high branch, Jack saw a town. Perhaps there, he thought, he'd find some answers.

Jack rode the wind to a group of settlers warming themselves by a fire.

"Hello," he greeted. "Hello. Good evening."

The townspeople walked by Jack as if he wasn't there at all.

"Ma'am?" He stopped beside a woman. She didn't see him.

He asked a young boy, "Excuse me. Can you tell me where I am?" The boy ran right through Jack.

"Hello! Hello!" Jack shouted.

It was then Jack realized he was invisible. No one could hear him. His fear caused snow to fall.

Shaken, Jack returned to the forest. He knew his name was Jack Frost because the moon told

. so, but for a long time that was all he knew. .ars and years passed, and Jack still hoped that .omeday he'd discover why he'd been created and what he was meant to do.

Far away, a fortress was nestled in a hidden corner of a massive ice canyon. Santa Claus's palace was enormous, crowded, busy, noisy—and the world's best-kept secret.

Here, at the North Pole, Santa was called "North."

On one side of North's Workshop, his famous red jacket and matching cap cast long shadows across the floor. On the other side was the man himself, holding a chainsaw and standing in front of a large block of ice. North raised the chainsaw, revealing a tattoo along his forearm. It said "Naughty." He dug into the block of ice with the chainsaw. Sharp bits of frozen water splattered throughout the Workshop.

Three elves stood in the doorway, munching on cookies meant for North.

"Still waiting for cookies!" North's deep,

Russian-accented voice boomed throughout t.
vast space of his workshop, reminding his elve.
that he was hungry for his snack.

His little helpers scooted out of the way as
North flopped back into his rolling chair and then
reached out toward a rack of work tools.

North grabbed a tiny hammer and then pushed
up his sleeves. On his other arm there was another
tattoo. This one read "Nice."

With delicate tools, North made a few final
cuts into the ice block. When the sculpture was
complete, North raised the frozen locomotive
he'd created and placed it carefully on a frozen
track. The train roared to life, belching chilly
vapor before chugging away.

North took a cookie. He watched his toy
hit a loop and then launch into the air. Wings
unfolded from the ice and a jet engine sizzled to
action.

But then the door to the Workshop burst open
with a heavy bang and crashed into the flying train.
A huge, hairy, abominable snowman flung himself
into the room. The yeti had a worried expression
across his furry brow. The ice train crashed to the

ground and then slid across the floor in a million pieces.

North was looking at the toy, shaking his head when the yeti began to shout.

"Arghbal . . ."

"How many times have I told you to knock?" North asked, spinning to face the huge beast.

"Warga blarghgha!" the yeti replied.

"What?" North said as he jumped up. "The Globe?" He drew his sword from its sheath, rushing from the room.

North pushed through a crowd of panicking elves. The bells on their hats jingled as North passed by. Yeti workers moved to the side.

"Shoo, with your pointy heads!" North called out to the elves. "Why are you always underboot?"

With large, quick steps he made his way to the Globe of Belief. The Globe sat in the center of his fortress. It was massive and covered with blazing lights. Tiny bulbs blanketed every continent.

"What is this?" North asked the yeti who had reported the problem. Hundreds of lights were dark. Squinting at the Globe, North was shocked as more and more lights turned off. It was as if someone, or some*thing*, was shutting them down by the thousands.

"Have you checked the axis?" North asked the yeti. "Is the rotation balanced?"

The yeti nodded. "Wardle bawddrel."

Wind began to blow into the large room. A blanket of black sand crept over the lights, snuffing them out in large blocks, until the entire Globe went black.

The elves began to scream. Gritty darkness swirled off the Globe and filled the room. It gathered into a tornado. The tornado rose up toward the ceiling, where it finally burst into a puff of smoke and disappeared.

The room settled into silence. No one dared move.

The Globe lights came back on, and everything seemed to return to normal . . . until the shadow appeared. Long and dark, the shadow of a man flashed across the floor before disappearing with an echoing laugh.

North stared at the place where the shadow had disappeared. "Can it be?" he muttered. He called to one of his elves, "Dingle!"

The elf appeared at North's side.

"Make preparations," North directed. "We are going to have company!"

The elf nodded as North reached out to grasp a large lever. It was for emergencies only. He twisted a dial and pulled down hard. The Globe began to glow. Then a beam of light zoomed up the axis shaft, toward the roof, and out into the world.

For the first time in decades, North had summoned the Guardians.

A little fairy flew above the head of a child who was fast asleep in bed. The fairy ducked under the pillow and came out the other side with a tooth in her tiny hand, leaving a coin behind. Then she returned to Tooth's glamorous palace within a hollowed-out mountain.

Hundreds of fairies were flitting outside the castle walls, either returning from similar missions or heading out to gather newly lost teeth.

Inside the castle, the little fairy handed in the tooth and was given another coin and house address. In the center of all this activity was the Tooth Fairy herself. Half human, half humming-bird, Tooth was beautiful, with brightly colored feathers and delicate wings that flapped excitedly as she shouted orders.

"Moscow, Sector 9—twenty-two incisors, eighteen premolars. Uh-oh, heavy rain advisory!" She paused to check the map. "Des Moines, we've got a cuspid at 23 Maple. Head out!"

"Wait!" Tooth suddenly cried. All work halted. Holding a single tooth in the air, she turned around to face her many Mini Fairies. Her shimmery wings flapped with excitement.

"It's her first tooth. Have you ever seen a more adorable lateral incisor in all your life?" Tooth gasped. "Look how she flossed."

The Mini Fairies nodded happily, tweeting with excitement and then with concern as they noticed a light filling the sky, stretching toward the castle and beyond. With a worried gulp of air, Tooth gathered her most trusted fairy advisers and then took off like a rocket.

A sleeping child was dreaming of playing soccer. His dream swirled above his head in a mist of fine golden sand. This stream of dreamsand was just one of many being sent out from the Sandman. From high up in the clouds, Sandy controlled the

dreams, sending those magical golden threads t
each child as he or she slept soundly.

His work brought him great joy. Sandy was
patting his round belly with a sense of satisfaction
when North's emergency signal zipped by. His joy
turned to concern.

In a flash, Sandy gathered the dreamsand
around him and then created a small plane.
Snuggling down into the cockpit, Sandy set a
course for due north and off he went.

Bunny, the Easter Bunny, ran through the sub-
terranean tunnel as fast as his floppy feet could
carry him. Easter eggs with little legs hopped
out of his way. He was six feet tall and had to
be careful not to bump his head while rushing.
Bunny popped out of the tunnels through a
rabbit hole at the North Pole and climbed up a
snowbank.

"Ah, it's freezing," Bunny complained. He
slogged through the wet and cold terrain, mutter-
ing to himself. "I can't feel my feet. I can't feel
my feet." He hopped quickly from one foot to the

er, over and over, until he finally reached the warmth of North's fortress.

They met in the Globe Room. As they waited for Sandy to arrive, North offered cookies and eggnog to Bunny and Tooth. As always, Tooth was busy directing her fairies to new teeth.

"This better be good, North," said Bunny.

At that moment, Sandy appeared. His dreamsand plane dissipated as he floated down to the floor. Using images in dreamsand, Sandy tried to convey to North just how busy he was.

"I know, I know," said North. "But I obviously wouldn't have called you all here unless it was serious."

North cleared his throat. "My fellow Guardians," he began. "It is our job to watch over the children of the world and keep them safe. To bring wonder, hope, and dreams. And so, I've called us all here for one reason, and one reason only: The children are in danger. An enemy we have kept at bay for centuries has finally decided to strike back. We alone can stop him."

The four Guardians moved to the center of the room.

"The Boogeyman was here—at the pole," North explained.

Tooth couldn't believe what she was hearing. "Pitch? Pitch Black? Here?"

North nodded. "Yes! There was black sand covering the Globe. And then a shadow!"

Bunny was confused. "What do you mean black sand? I thought you said you saw Pitch."

"Well, ah, not exactly," North confessed.

Bunny was not amused. "'Not exactly'? Can you believe this guy?" He looked at Sandy, who gave a sympathetic shrug and formed a question mark with his dreamsand.

North continued, "Pitch is up to something very bad. I feel it in my belly."

"Hang on. You mean to say you summoned me here three days before Easter because of your belly?" asked Bunny. "Mate, if I did this to you three days before Christmas—"

Bunny was interrupted by Tooth giving more orders to her fairies. "Argentina. Priority alert! A batch of bicuspids in Buenos Aires."

"Please, Bunny. Easter is not Christmas," North added.

"Here we go," said Bunny, and then he laughed. "North, I don't have time for this. I've still got two million eggs to finish up."

"No matter how much you paint, it is still an egg," North countered.

While North and Bunny argued and Tooth continued to work, Sandy noticed that the moon had come into view through a window in the ceiling. The moon's rays shined brightly, filling the Globe Room with moonlight.

He tried to signal to the other Guardians with his dreamsand images, but they weren't paying attention.

"Come on, Pitch went out with the Dark Ages. We made sure of that, remember?" Bunny reminded North.

"I know it was him. We have a serious situation," North replied.

"Well, I've got a serious situation with some eggs," said Bunny.

Sandy didn't know what else to do, so he grabbed one of North's elves and began to shake him. The elf's bells rang throughout the room. The other Guardians finally stopped what they were doing. Sandy formed an image of a crescent moon above his head.

"Aah! The Man in the Moon!" exclaimed North. "Sandy, why didn't you say something?"

Sandy gave North a frustrated look. Dreamsand poured out of his ears.

North spoke to the moon. "It's been a long time, old friend. What is the big news?"

A beam of moonlight focused on a spot on the floor in the center of the four Guardians. Then the light shifted, darkening to shadows until it revealed a silhouette of Pitch. The Guardians continued to stare in disbelief.

"It *is* Pitch," Bunny said.

"Manny, what must we do?" asked North.

In response, the beam of moonlight grew brighter before shrinking to a thinner ray of light. At the center of the circle, the light illuminated an ornate symbol on the floor. The symbol rose out of the ground, revealing a large gem on top of a pillar.

North was awed as the gem refracted light throughout the chamber, like a crystal.

"Uh, guys, you know what this means?" Tooth asked the group with a gasp.

"He's choosing a new Guardian," North said.

Tooth nodded. "I wonder who it's gonna be."

Sandy created images with his dreamsand as Tooth began to guess who they might be adding to their exclusive group.

"Maybe the Leprechaun?" Tooth guessed.

"Please not the Groundhog, please not the Groundhog," Bunny chanted.

A sudden bright light flashed through the room. Above the glowing stone on the pillar, a holographic photo of a cloaked figure appeared. The figure held a hooked staff.

The Mini Fairies all sighed with delight as the Guardians stared, baffled by Manny's choice.

"Jack Frost," North muttered.

"Ah, I take it all back!" Bunny whimpered. "The Groundhog's fine!"

"Well, ah, as long as he helps to, ah . . . protect the children, right?" Tooth stammered.

But Bunny couldn't—wouldn't—believe it. "Jack Frost? He doesn't care about children! All he does is freeze water pipes and mess with my egg hunts. Right? He's an irresponsible, selfish—"

"Guardian," North interrupted.

Bunny shook his head. "Jack Frost is many things, but he is *not* a Guardian!"

Jack Frost sat on top of a post office box in St. Petersburg, Russia, ready to make trouble. He touched the end of his staff down to the ground, which sent frost streaking across the street.

A Russian boy was taking a drink from a water fountain when the water froze midstream. His lips stuck to the icy spray. "Ahhh!" he screamed, unable to move.

A mailman came to help, but out of nowhere a patch of ice appeared under his feet. *Boom!* The man fell right down on his bottom.

The streak of frost continued up a rainspout. The windows of an apartment building frosted over.

Inside, a goldfish swam to the surface of its bowl to eat, but a thin layer of ice coated the top of the water, blocking the food. In the next room a writer sat next to a stack of papers. A sudden gust of wind blew his pages out the window. As the ice moved along the walls of the building, it froze power lines and clotheslines.

Jack Frost climbed to a high point in the city to see what his frost had done.

He smiled. "Ah, now *that* was fun. Hey, wind!" The trees began to sway, and leaves flew into the air. Jack gathered the gusts. "Take me home." The wind lifted him up, carrying him away from Russia.

"Wooooo-hoooooo!" Jack shouted in joy as he flew away.

When he arrived home, Jack decided to give a gift to the town of Burgess. Springtime was almost here, but there was still time for one more . . .

"SNOW DAY!" Jack jumped off his windy ride and landed in the town's center. He zoomed through the streets, forcing people to wrap themselves tightly in their jackets.

A boy named Jamie was walking home when Jack's wind ripped his book out of his hands. The book was called *They're Out There—Mysteries, Mythical Creatures, and the Unexplained Phenomena.*

As Jamie grabbed it back, Jack zoomed up next to him. He said, "Huh, that looks interesting. Good book?"

Jamie couldn't see or hear Jack, so he continued walking.

Claude and Caleb, twin boys in Jamie's grade, came rushing by. They were pushing each other and laughing as they went.

"All right! Yeah!" Claude cheered.

"Wahoo! Snow day!" Caleb hooted before shoving his brother into a snowdrift.

Jack grinned and then said, "You're welcome!" But like Jamie, they couldn't see or hear Jack Frost.

Jamie ran after the twins. "Hey, guys, wait up. Are you guys coming to the egg hunt on Sunday?"

"Yeah, free candy!" answered Caleb.

"I hope we can find the eggs with all this snow!" added Claude.

The three boys soon reached Jamie's house. Jamie showed the twins his book. Jack watched them from his perch on the fence.

"Whoa," Jamie told his friends, "it says here

that they found Bigfoot hair samples and DNA in Michigan. That's, like, superclose."

"Here we go again," Claude said with a moan.

Jamie looked at his two-year-old sister, Sophie, playing in their front yard. She was wearing fairy wings and trying to ride on their large greyhound dog.

"You saw the video too, Claude. He's out there." Jamie entered the gate while the boys stood by the fence and waited.

Caleb chuckled. "That's what you said about aliens."

"And the Easter Bunny," Claude added.

Jamie grabbed his sled from the porch. "The Easter Bunny *is* real."

"Oh, the Easter Bunny's real, all right. Real annoying, real grumpy, and *really* full of himself," Jack said, even though he knew the boys couldn't hear him.

Claude giggled. "Come on, you guys believe anything."

Sophie got into the fun. "Easter Bunny!" She giggled. "Hop, hop, hop!" Sophie fell over from hopping. "Ow."

"Mom!" Jamie called into the house. "Sophie fell again."

Jamie's Mom came outside to see what was going on. "You okay, Soph?" She picked up her daughter and then dusted off the snow.

Caleb asked Jamie, "Are we sledding or what?"

At that, Jamie's Mom said, "Jamie, hat? We don't want Jack Frost nipping at your nose." She handed Jamie his cap.

"Who's Jack Frost?" Jamie asked his mother.

Jamie's Mom smiled. "No one, honey. It's just an expression."

"Hey!" Jack was offended. He gathered a perfect snowball off the ground. He stared at it and imitated Jamie, saying, *"Who's Jack Frost?"* He blew on the snowball. It turned a magical shade of blue.

Jack faced Jamie, took aim, and . . . direct hit!

"Who threw that?" Jamie glanced around, laughing. He leaped into a group of kids playing in the snow.

"It wasn't Bigfoot, kiddo," Jack replied with a smile.

Jamie looked around for the snowball thrower.

He found a couple of kids making a barricade and tossed a snowball at them.

The snowball hit a kid named Monty in the head, knocking off his thick glasses. Monty fell face-first into the snow. "Ow," he said as he struggled to get back up.

A girl named Pippa went to throw a snowball at Jamie when one of Jack's hit her. "Jamie Bennett! No fair!"

Jamie laughed. "You struck first!"

Before Pippa could respond, Jack hit Caleb in the side of the head with a snowball.

"Oh!" Claude giggled at his twin brother.

Jack was just warming up for the battle. "Free for all!" he shouted as he supplied the kids with snowballs. "All right, who needs ammo?"

"Ow." Monty got hit again.

"Look at that," Jack said, watching the battle.

Jamie was using his sled as a shield and was backing away when he bumped into a snowman. They both fell over.

Suddenly a snowball hit Cupcake in the back of the head. Cupcake was the toughest girl in their grade. Hands on her hips, Cupcake looked around, searching for the kid who tossed it.

"Grrrrrrrr," Cupcake growled.

The snowballs stopped flying as everyone turned to see what Cupcake would do.

Pippa shivered. "Crud, I hit Cupcake."

Monty pointed at Pippa. "She hit Cupcake."

Claude asked Pippa, "You hit Cupcake?"

Jamie was terrified. Cupcake was looking at him as if he'd been the one to throw the snowball. He was about to defend himself when another snowball pegged Cupcake. The kids all gasped in horror as the cold, wet snowball left a magical blue mark.

"Oh!" Claude said.

Caleb asked Monty, "Did you throw that?"

Monty shook his head. "No."

"Wasn't me," Pippa announced.

The moment was tense, but as Jack Frost's blue magic oozed from the snow, Cupcake's face turned from anger to joy. She began to laugh. Then Cupcake began a game of chase with the other kids. Jamie jumped up to join the fun while Jack ran along, enjoying the excitement.

As they reached the top of the hill, Jack said, "Ooh, little slippery!" He blasted a sheet of ice behind him. All the kids fell to the ground, except for Jamie, who landed on his sled.

"Whooaaaa!" Jamie shrieked as his sled began to slide down the sheet of ice.

"Whoaaa," Claude said.

"Jamie, watch out!" Pippa warned as Jamie flew by. His sled was picking up speed.

"Stop!" Caleb shouted.

But Jamie kept on sliding.

"Jamie, turn, turn!" Monty directed.

"That's the street!" Pippa cried out.

"What are you doing?" Caleb asked.

"Stop!" Claude shouted. "There's traffic!"

Jamie shot out from the trees and whooshed past a row of parked cars.

Jack's path of ice continued down the street, sending Jamie straight into the traffic Claude had warned about.

"Whoa!" Jamie cried as he barely missed a moving truck, sending furniture tumbling out of the back and causing a four-car pileup.

Jack glanced at the damage and called to Jamie, "Don't worry, kid. I gotcha."

Jamie, of course, couldn't hear Jack. He

became increasingly frightened as Jack shouted, "Hold on! It's gonna be all right."

"Ahhh!" Jamie's sled was sliding faster and faster. "No, no, no, no. . . ." He narrowly missed hitting people in the crosswalk and dodged a couple walking their dog.

Jack threw out more ice, sending Jamie onto the sidewalk. "Keep up with me, kid! Take a left."

A pedestrian told Jamie, "Slow down!"

Jamie was out of control. "Whoa, whoa, whoa, whoa!"

"Is that Jamie Bennett?" a woman asked her friend as Jamie zoomed by.

The friend replied with a shout to Jamie, "Hey! Watch it!"

A guy pointed in awe. "Look at that dude!"

Jamie flew off the sidewalk and back into the street. He nearly knocked down the mail carrier.

Jack looked at Jamie. Jamie's face was full of fear, but there was also excitement in his eyes. The ride was fun, and Jack knew it. He turned the sled to protect Jamie from an oncoming snowplow, then changed the pathway of the ice trail. Jamie's sled turned onto a newly formed ice ramp.

"AAAAHHHHHHH!" Jamie shouted as he rode the ramp and launched into the air. His sled traveled over the statue of the town's founder, Thaddeus Burgess.

Jamie landed safely in the snow on the other side with a bump and a skid.

Jamie's friends ran over to make certain he had survived.

"Oh my gosh!" Pippa exclaimed.

Jack stood atop the statue. He was pleased. "Yeah!"

"Jamie!" Claude shouted.

"Wow, that looks serious, Jamie." Caleb checked out the landing site.

"Jamie, are you all right?" Pippa asked.

"Is he okay?" Monty wondered.

Jamie leaped up from the sled. He wasn't hurt, not even a scratch. "Whoaaa!" he said, excitedly. "Did you guys see that? It was amazing. I did a jump and slid under a—" A sofa that had flown out of the furniture truck skidded past and came to a stop, pushing Jamie over as it went.

"Whoops!" said Jack.

Claude cringed. "Ooooh!"

The kids waited to see if Jamie survived a sec-nd time. He slowly rose from behind the sofa, grinning. There was a new hole in his smile, and Jamie held up his tooth.

Jamie showed the others. "Cool! A tooth!"

"Dude!" Claude said. "That means cash."

Caleb was jealous. "Tooth Fairy cash!"

Pippa said, "I love the Tooth Fairy."

Jack Frost was bummed. The Tooth Fairy had just stolen all his glory. "Oh no. . . ," He moaned.

"That's totally awesome," Monty said.

"You lucky bug!" Claude said.

"Lucky," Caleb agreed.

"No!" Jack Frost shook his head. The day's adventure was his, *not* the Tooth Fairy's.

"I gotta put this under my pillow." Jamie held his tooth very carefully.

"I wish I lost my tooth," Caleb and Pippa said at the same time.

Jack was mad. "Ah, wait a minute! Come on. Hold on. Hold *on*! What about all that fun we just had? That wasn't the Tooth Fairy, that was me!"

Claude said, "I lost two teeth in one day once. Remember that?"

"What are you gonna buy?" Cupcake asked Jan

"How much do you think she's going to leave? Caleb asked.

Jack looked at the kids, and his frustration grew. Storm clouds gathered above his head and began to darken. The sky rumbled. Snow flurries started to fall.

"Let's go," Pippa told the others. "I'm cold."

Claude looked at Jamie. "What *are* you gonna spend your money on?"

"My ears are freezing," Caleb complained as the temperature continued to drop.

"I can't feel my toes," added Claude. "It's hot cocoa time."

Jack jumped down from the statue, still trying to remind the kids about the good time they'd had in the snow. But because the kids couldn't see or hear him, one by one they left for home.

Jumping in front of Jamie, Jack tried to block his way. "What's a guy gotta do to get a little attention around here?" Jack muttered.

Whoosh. Jamie dashed through Jack.

Jack was shaken for a second. By the time he looked around, the kids had disappeared and he

s alone on the street. He sat back, feeling the
hilly change in the weather that he'd created.
Then, gathering the wind for a ride, Jack lifted
himself up and soared over the town.

CHAPTER FOUR

Jamie was in his bedroom, playing with a toy robot. Behind his head, drawings of UFOs, aliens, Bigfoot, and other mythical creatures were pinned to the wall. When he got home that afternoon, Jamie had made a drawing of himself flying midair on his sled. Now it was hanging on the wall too.

"I did this jump and it was amazing, and I slid under a car and it was awesome." Jamie was telling the day's adventure to his mom and Sophie. "Then I was flying down this hill, and I was like, *whoosh, whoosh, whoosh* through all these cars, and then the sled hit this . . . this *thing*, and I was, like, way up in the air."

Jamie used the robot to show his mom how he flew. Sophie and the dog sat on the floor, paying attention to the whole story.

"And then *bam*! Then the sofa hit me, and see?" He opened wide and explained how the tooth fell out. "Ah hoo hay ow!"

Sophie jumped up. She tried to put her finger into Jamie's mouth.

Jamie's Mom pulled Sophie back. "All right, you," she said to Jamie. "Tooth under your pillow?"

Jamie placed his robot on the nightstand and then reached for his favorite stuffed rabbit.

"Yeah," Jamie told his mom with a satisfied smile. "I'm ready." Under his pillow were the tooth, a camera, and a flashlight.

She saw the look of anticipation on his face and warned, "Now, don't stay up trying to see her, Jamie, or she won't come."

"But I can do it this time," Jamie assured his mother. "You want to help me, Soph? We can hide and see the Tooth Fairy!"

Sophie began running around the room. "Hide! Hide, hide, hide . . ."

Jamie's Mom gathered Sophie into her arms. The dog began licking Jamie's face.

His mother shook her head. "Straight to bed now, mister."

"Mom," Jamie whined.

But Jamie's Mom was serious about bedtim She carried Sophie into the hall, closing Jamie': door behind them.

Jack Frost was hanging upside down outside Jamie's window. His cool breath frosted over the glass. The full moon above him lit up the sky.

"If there's something I'm doing wrong, I'd really like to know what it is," he said to the moon. "'Cause I've tried *everything*, and no one ever sees me." The moon remained silent. "I mean, you put me here, the least you can do is tell me *why*."

The moon continued to shine, steady and unchanging.

Jack shook his head and grumbled, "Why do I bother?"

He moved away from Jamie's window, jumping onto a telephone pole. As he walked along the wires, a stream of dreamsand zipped behind his head. Then another in front of him. Strands of dreamsand surrounded Jack on their way into the bedroom windows of sleeping children.

Jack smiled. "Right on time, Sandman."

Jack ran along the telephone wire until he caught up to a strand and then began to follow it. Behind him, another stream of dreamsand morphed into a dolphin and entered a nearby window. And yet another swooped downward into Cupcake's room.

Cupcake was fast asleep. She held a stuffed unicorn while her dreams swirled above her head. She was imagining a story about a little girl riding a unicorn. In her dream, the unicorn was dashing around her room.

When the room began to darken, sleeping Cupcake didn't stir. A shadowy figure rose from under her bed.

Pitch, the Boogeyman, was there. Hiding. Waiting. And now he was ready for action.

He laughed a sinister chuckle as he studied Cupcake's happy little dream. "Ohhhh," he mocked. "I thought I heard the *clippity-clop* of a unicorn. What an adorable dream!" His frowning lips curled into a small grin. "And look at her. Precious child. So sweet, so full of hope and wonder." Pitch raised his eyebrows. "Why, there's only one thing missing. . . . A touch of fear."

Pitch touched a bony finger to the unicorn in Cupcake's dream. The creature turned black and then shriveled before melting into nothingness. Cupcake flinched in her sleep.

"Ha, ha, ha! That never gets old." Pitch snickered. He raised his finger again and swirled the dreamsand around Cupcake's bed. It turned into black nightmare sand.

"Feel your fear," Pitch told Cupcake. "Come on, come on." He watched her toss and turn. "That's right."

The black sand gathered and formed into a bucking horse. A Nightmare had taken shape.

"Yessss," Pitch hissed. "What a pretty little Nightmare. Now"—he turned to the scary, dark horse—"I want you to tell the others, the wait is over." Pitch tossed the Nightmare out the window, where it met up with other Nightmares gathering on the streets. They all flew off together, away from town.

Pitch stepped out of Cupcake's room and watched them go. He walked in a crooked line, careful to avoid any beams of moonlight. From the shadows, Pitch glanced up at the moon and said, "Don't look at me like that, Old Man. My Nightmares are finally ready. Are your Guardians?"

"Whoa!" Jack Frost was walking high above town, watching dreamsand streams slip silently into a row of homes when suddenly a shadowy figure ran past him. Jack leaped down from the wire to investigate. At first all he heard were the voices of townspeople preparing to go inside for the night.

A man asked his wife, "Did you leave the windows open again?"

Jack didn't hear the reply, but a person in another house said, "The garage door is wide open."

He wandered past the houses, still searching for the shadowy figure. Once again, something zoomed by him. He couldn't see what it was, so Jack jumped onto the roof of a truck for a better view.

Whoosh. There it went again. A trash can tumbled over. Jack hopped down from the truck and then scooted backward into a dark alley.

"Hello, mate."

Jack spun to face the owner of the voice. He squinted as Bunny stepped fully into the light.

Bunny spoke first. "Been a long time. Blizzard of '68, I believe? Easter Sunday, wasn't it?"

Jack's jaw dropped. "Bunny? You're not still mad about *that*, are you?"

"Yes," Bunny answered simply. "But this is about something else." He glanced around the alley, calling, "Fellas."

Before Jack could react, a huge hairy hand reached forward and then lifted him off the ground.

"Hey!" Jack protested.

"Durbha wahla," one yeti said as a second yeti took hold of Jack's arms.

"Put me down," Jack insisted.

The yetis shoved Jack into a sack. The first yeti took out a snow globe and then smashed it on the ground, saying, "Durtal bardla burdlew." A magic portal opened in front of them.

The yetis indicated that Bunny should go first, saying, "Dward urghwetee."

"Me?" Bunny pointed to himself. "Not on your nelly. See you back at the Pole."

And with that, Bunny stomped his big foot on the ground. A rabbit hole appeared, and Bunny jumped into it.

"Bwardla arghl," a yeti said before tossing Jack into the snow globe portal.

"Ahhhhhhh!" Jack's voice echoed as he fell. The two yetis leaped in after him.

Tooth was running her business from North's fortress. "Tangiers! 421 rue de Barat! *Allez!*" She sent a Mini Fairy to get a tooth from that address.

Suddenly a sack flew out of a portal and thudded onto the floor.

"He's here," North announced.

Crawling out of the bag, Jack found North and Sandy staring at him. Tooth was nearby, surrounded by a dozen hovering Mini Fairies who came and went as she barked orders at them.

"Walla Walla, Washington, we've got a trampoline mishap at 1340 Ginger Lane," she told a fairy. "Canine, lateral, *and* central incisor. Ouch!" The little fairy hurried away.

North cleared his throat. "There he is." He pointed and announced, "Jack Frost." Raising his arms, he welcomed Jack. Sandy made a snowflake out of dreamsand appear above his head.

"Wow. You've *got* to be kidding me," said Jack. The two yetis reached forward and propped him up. "Hey, hey. Whoa, put me down."

"I hope the yctis treated you well," North said.

"Oh, yeah," Jack replied, sarcastically. "I love being shoved in a sack and tossed through a magic portal."

"Oh good." North nodded. "That was *my* idea." Bunny entered the room and North said, "You know Bunny, obviously."

"Obviously," Jack replied.

Bunny stood to the side, with his arms crossed, while the Mini Fairies swarmed around Jack.

"And the Tooth Fairy." North made the introduction.

Before Jack could answer, Tooth glided toward him. "Hello, Jack," she greeted. "I've heard a lot about you. And your teeth."

Jack put a hand to his mouth. "My . . . my what?"

Tooth leaned in way too close. "Open up," she said. "Are they really as white as they say?" She was very excited. "Yes!" Tooth gasped. "Oh, they really do sparkle like freshly fallen snow."

Several of the Mini Fairies began to flutter like butterflies around Jack's face, trying to get a look in his mouth.

"Girls, pull yourselves together. Let's not disgrace the uniform." Tooth ordered them all back.

North went on with the introductions. "And Sandman." The dream maker had fallen asleep. North shook him. "Sandy! Sandy! Wake up."

Sandy bolted upright and then smiled at Jack.

"Anyone want to tell me why I'm here?" Jack was getting impatient.

Sandy made dreamsand images appear over his head.

"That's not really helping," Jack told him. "But thanks, little man." To the others he said, "I musta done something *really* bad to get *you* four together." Jack walked around the room, stopping before North. "Am I on the naughty list?"

North laughed so hard, his belly shook. "On the naughty list? You hold the record!" He became serious. "But no matter. We overlook. Now we are wiping clean the slate," he said, mixing up the phrase, like he so often did.

"How come?" Jack asked.

"Good question," Bunny said.

"How come?" North repeated. "I'll tell you how come." He turned to Jack. "Because now you are a Guardian."

While Jack stood there entirely confused, the yetis lit ceremonial torches. Elves leaped down from columns, unfurling banners as they descended. A few of the Mini Fairies brought Jack flowers, which he refused to take.

"What are you doing?" Jack pushed the fairies back. "Get off of me."

Horns blared throughout the room.

"This is the best part," North told Jack.

An elf marching band entered the room while the yetis pushed Jack to his designated spot on the floor. More elves brought in a pair of ceremonial boots.

A yeti handed North a thick book. He blew off the dust and then began searching for the correct page.

Jack slammed his staff on the floor. Frost and wind blasted throughout the room. Everyone stopped as the torches blew out.

"What makes you think I would want to be a Guardian?" Jack asked.

North looked at Jack and chuckled. "Of course you do." He cued the elf band to start playing again. "Music!"

"No music!" Jack shouted. The band gave up, and with a huff one of the elves tossed his trumpet onto the ground and stomped out of the room. "Look," Jack said to the Guardians, "this is all very flattering, but, ah, you don't want me. You're all hard work and deadlines, and I'm snowballs and fun times. I'm not a Guardian."

"That's exactly what I said!" Bunny agreed.

Tooth flew toward Jack. "Jack, I don't think you understand what it is we do." She told Jack to look at the massive Globe behind him. "Each of those lights is a child," Tooth began.

North picked up the story. "A child who believes. And good or bad, naughty or nice, we protect them." Then he added, "Tooth, fingers out of mouth."

Tooth was once again examining Jack's teeth. She couldn't help herself. "Oh, sorry. They're beautiful." She blushed.

North went on, saying, "Okay, no more wishy-washy! Pitch is out there doing who knows what!"

"You mean the Boogeyman?" Jack snickered.

"Yes!" North said. "When Pitch threatens *us*, he threatens *them* as well." North pointed at the Globe.

"All the more reason to pick someone more qualified," Jack said.

"Pick?" North was frustrated. "You think *we* pick? No, you were *chosen*, like we were *all* chosen. By the Man in the Moon."

That caught Jack's attention. "What?" he asked.

"Last night, Jack," Tooth said. "He chose you."

Bunny snorted. "Maybe."

Jack squinted at North. "The Man in the Moon? He talks to you?"

"You see, you cannot say no," North said. "It is destiny."

Feeling like his head might burst from too much information, Jack asked, "But why wouldn't he tell me about that himself?" He sighed. "After three hundred years, this is his answer. To spend *eternity* like you guys, cooped up in some hideout, thinking of new ways to bribe kids? No, that's *not* for me. No offense."

"How's that not offensive?" Bunny sneered. "You know what I think? I think we just dodged a bullet. I mean, what's this clown know about bringing joy to children, anyway?"

Jack felt like he had to defend himself. "Uh, you ever hear of a snow day? I know it's no hard-boiled egg, but kids *like* what I do."

Bunny replied, "But none of them believe in you." He leaned in toward Jack and then said softly, "Do they? You see, you're invisible, mate. It's like you don't even exist."

"Bunny! Enough!" Tooth flitted between Bunny and Jack.

"No, the kangaroo's right," Jack said.

Bunny glared at him. "The . . . the what? What'd you call me? I am *not* a *kangaroo*, mate."

"Oh." Jack scoffed. "And this whole time I though you were. If you're not a kangaroo, what are you?"

"I'm a bunny!" Bunny said. "The Easter Bunny. People believe in me."

North stepped forward. "Jack," he said, interrupting the argument. "Walk with me."

North led Jack into an elevator that looked like a Christmas tree ornament. When the door opened, they stepped out into North's Factory.

Jack took in the yetis, elves, and toys. He said, "It's nothing personal, North. What you all do . . . It's just . . . It's not my thing."

North replied, "The Man in the Moon says it is your thing. We will see."

With big footsteps, North hurried through the factory. Jack struggled to keep up. He was distracted by everything he saw.

"Slow down, wouldja?" Jack said, panting. "I've been trying to bust in here for years, I want a good look."

North refused to slow. "What do you mean, 'bust in'?"

"Oh, don't worry," Jack replied. "I never got past the yetis."

A yeti nearby pounded his fist into his palm and growled a warning. "Rwwarrrrr."

Jack grinned. "Oh, hey, Phil."

North was impatient with Jack's antics. "Keep up, Jack! Keep up!"

Jack tried to keep pace, but there was so much to look at. Yetis were building toys and moving packages while elves were test-piloting flying machines.

"Whoa!" Jack dodged a duck toy. "I always thought the elves made the toys."

"We just let them believe that," said North. Then he glanced over his shoulder. Jack followed his gaze to see elves eating tinsel. "Very nice! Keep up the good work!" North encouraged.

As they went deeper into the factory, yetis and elves brought North toys for inspection. One yeti held out a blue robot. "I don't like it," North said. "Paint it red." Then in a booming voice, he announced, "Step it up, everybody."

As the factory roared with increased energy, North and Jack entered North's Workshop.

North's shelves were filled with sketches, par̶
and toys. There were blocks of ice on his work̶
bench from which he carved toy prototypes.

When North rolled up his sleeves, Jack could see
the Naughty and Nice tattoos. North took a plate
from an elf and offered Jack a slice of fruitcake.

"Ah, no, thanks," Jack refused.

North threw the plate across the room. It
slammed into the wall with a crash. He then stared
with hooded eyes at Jack. "Now we get down to
tacks of brass," North said with a growl.

"'Tacks of brass'?" Jack repeated softly to
himself.

North cracked his knuckles, and Jack stopped
talking. A gust of wind closed the office door, and
the door locked itself. North moved closer toward
Jack. With each step forward, Jack stepped backward until he was pressed against the locked door.

"Who are you, Jack Frost?" North asked. "What
is your center?" He poked Jack in the chest.

Jack looked down at North's thick finger and
asked, "My *center*?"

"If the Man in the Moon chose *you* to be a
Guardian, you must have something very special

side," North said. "Hmmm." He picked up a set of Russian nesting dolls, carved into his likeness.

"Here," he told Jack. "This is how you see me, no? Very big, intimidating. But if you get to know me a little . . ." He handed the doll to Jack. "Well, go on."

With a curious expression, Jack set aside his staff and then opened the first doll. Inside was another North doll. This one was a cheery Santa Claus with red cheeks.

"You are downright jolly," Jack commented.

"Ah," North said. "But not *just* jolly . . ." He encouraged Jack to continue to open the dolls. Each one got smaller and smaller as Jack removed them. They were all versions of North, but slightly different.

"I am also mysterious," North said, pointing to one doll. "And fearless." He pointed to another. "And caring." One more to go. "And at my center . . ."

The smallest doll was no bigger than a jellybean.

"There's a tiny wooden baby?" Jack joked.

"Look closer. What do you see?" North asked.

"You have big eyes?" Jack guessed.

"Yes!" North beamed. "Big eyes. *Very b*▨
Because they are full of *wonder*. That is my center
It is what I was born with. Eyes that have always
seen the wonder in *everything*!"

With a wave of his arms, the toys on North's
shelves burst to life. Jack-in-the-boxes popped.
Trains sped around the room. Soldiers began to
march. Toy planes zoomed around. An elf was
lifted and carried by a balloon.

"Eyes that see lights in the trees and magic
in the air." A toy plane stalled in front of North
before taking flight again. "This wonder is what I
put into the world and what I protect in children.
It is what makes me a Guardian. It is my center."
North looked to Jack. "What is yours?"

"I don't know." Jack stared down at the tiny
wooden Santa in his palm. North reached out and
then closed Jack's palm around the doll, silently
telling him to keep it.

Suddenly, Bunny came running up.

"We have a problem, mate," Bunny announced
in a panicked rush. "Trouble at the Tooth Palace."

North immediately led Bunny, Sandy, and Jack
to the sleigh hangar. Tooth had already gone ahead

to her palace. Several yetis rushed in to prepare the sleigh for launch.

"Boys, shipshape," North told the yetis. "As soon as impossible."

Jack stepped out of the way as a yeti hurried by. "North, North!" He called for North's attention. "I told you, I'm not going with you guys. There's no way I'm climbing into some rickety old—" The sound of pounding hooves and snorting reindeer cut him off.

The sleigh was incredible. It was huge and shining. This was not just a sleigh—it was a totally tricked-out, hot rod of a sleigh, complete with all kinds of gadgets. "Whoa" was all Jack could manage to say.

North called the massive reindeer to a halt.

The sleigh stopped, and the yetis finished preparations for takeoff.

"Okay," Jack said. He was dying to get inside and check out the sleigh. "One ride. But that's it." Jack jumped in.

"Everyone loves the sleigh." North gave a smile and a nod to Sandy, who then climbed into his own spot in the back. Taking the reins, North wrapped them around his powerful arms, then turned to

Bunny, who was still standing outside the sleigh.

"Bunny, what are you waiting for?" North asked.

"I think my tunnels might be faster, mate," Bunny said. "And, um, safer."

North reached out and hauled Bunny aboard. "Ah, get in. Buckle up."

Bunny looked frantically around the seat. "Whoa, whoa, whoa. Where are the seat belts?"

North laughed. "That was just an expression." He asked the yetis, "Are we ready?"

One yeti shook his head, but North ignored him and cracked the reins. "Good!" he shouted. "Let's go! Clear!"

Elves and yetis scattered as the sleigh headed down a long sledding track. North and Jack were enjoying the speed, while Bunny cowered against Sandy.

"Out of the way!" North shouted to a few elves as they passed. "Hyah!" He shook the reins, and the reindeer picked up the pace.

The sleigh went straight up for a few minutes, then zoomed straight down. Sandy grinned and Jack shouted in delight. North pulled a lever, sending the sleigh into a corkscrew. "I hope you like the loopty-loops!"

Bunny turned green. "I hope you like carrots," he said, threatening to throw up his lunch.

"Here we go!" North said. The sleigh reached the bottom of the track and shot off the ramp at the end, up and out into the bright blue sky.

"Wooo-hooooo!!!!" Jack raised his arms in the air.

"Klassno!" North told the reindeer.

Jack leaped to the rear of the sled to see the North Pole disappear as they sped through the sky. "Hey, Bunny." Jack stood dangerously on the back edge of the sleigh. "Check out the view." Suddenly, Jack flipped off the side. "EEEYAAAAGGGGHHH!"

Bunny gasped and gingerly peered over the side, thinking Jack had fallen, only to find Jack lounging on the sleigh's skid. "Aww. You *do* care," Jack said with a smile.

Bunny scowled at Jack while Jack climbed back into his seat.

North rattled the reins. "Hold on, everyone. I know a shortcut!"

Bunny groaned. "I knew we should have taken the tunnels."

North held up a snow globe. "Tooth Palace," he told the globe. An image of Tooth's castle filled the globe. North tossed the snow globe in front of the sleigh, and a giant portal opened in the sky.

"Hyah!" North shouted. The sleigh was sucked through the vortex.

The sleigh emerged outside the Tooth Palace. Streaks of black filled the sky around the beautiful, delicate castle.

"What?!" North squinted. "What are they?"

On closer look, Jack could see that the streaks were horses made of black sand. Nightmares. Mini Fairies flew past the sleigh, screaming in horror.

Sandy and Bunny ducked as Nightmares swooped by the sled.

"Whoa!" Bunny shouted.

"They're taking the Mini Fairies!" Jack pointed to a stream of Nightmares chasing a pack of fairies and gulping them down into the blackness. A lone fairy was flying nearby with a big ugly Nightmare at her heels. Jack reached out and rescued her before the Nightmare could swallow her up.

"Hey, little Baby Tooth," Jack said. "You okay?" He held her safely away from the Nightmares.

Baby Tooth nodded as North drove the sleigh through the Tooth Palace. There were pillars as far as the eye could see. Each pillar contained millions of boxes where baby teeth were stored.

Inside the chamber, North handed the sleigh reins to Jack.

"Here," he said. "Take over."

"Huh?" Bunny asked.

"Hyah!" Jack said, gladly taking control.

North unsheathed his swords and slashed a Nightmare in half. "Yah!" he shouted as the Nightmare split open and hundreds of tooth boxes spilled down into the sleigh. The Nightmare disintegrated.

"They're stealing the teeth!" Bunny cried.

Sandy looked at where the Nightmare disappeared. The Nightmare had become grains of black sand that were now attaching to one another. Within seconds, a new Nightmare was created.

The Guardians looked up just as Jack was about to plow the sleigh into one of the pillars.

"Jack! Look out!" North shouted.

Jack pulled back the reins. "Aaahhh!" The sleigh sideswiped the pillar and then landed hard on a platform. Tooth was directly above the Guardians' heads.

"Tooth!" North called out. "Are you all right?"

Tooth was flying in circles, frustrated and angry. "They took my fairies!" she shrieked. "And the teeth! All of them! Everything is gone! *Everything!*" Defeated, her wings began to droop.

The Guardians gathered around. Baby Tooth popped out of Jack's coat hood and then flew to Tooth.

"Oh, thank goodness! One of you is all right!" Tooth raised her damp eyes to the fairy.

Pitch's voice boomed through the cavernous room. "I have to say, this is very, very exciting." He was standing above them with a smug smile. "The big four. All in one place. I'm a little starstruck." His chuckle echoed. "Did you like my show on the Globe, North?" But before North could reply, he said, "Got you all together, didn't I?"

"Pitch!" Tooth demanded. "You have got thirty seconds to return my fairies!"

"Or what?" Pitch's voice boomed as he darted back into the shadows.

Tooth followed the echo and found him near one of her tooth box columns.

"You'll stick a quarter under my pillow?" Pitch mocked before disappearing again.

"Why are you doing this?" North asked.

With the speed and effortlessness of a shadow, Pitch had moved to the other side of the palace. He slowly traveled to the center of the chamber.

"Maybe I want what you have," he said. "To be believed in. Maybe I'm tired of hiding under beds."

"Maybe that's where you belong," Bunny suggested.

"Ah, go suck an egg, rabbit," Pitch replied.

Bunny looked over the side of the platform where he was standing to see Pitch there, hanging upside down. Pitch winked at Bunny, then moved away.

"Hang on, is that Jack Frost?" Pitch asked, laughing. "Since when are you all so chummy?"

"We're not," Jack replied.

"Oh good," Pitch told him. Jack turned to find

Pitch standing nearby. "A neutral party. Then i
going to ignore you. But you must be used to th
by now."

Bunny was angry. "Pitch! You shadow-sneaking
ratbag! Come here!"

Bunny leaped after Pitch, but he once more disappeared and reappeared elsewhere. Tooth spotted
him first. She grabbed one of Bunny's boomerangs
and then flew at Pitch in a rage. "Ahhhhhh!"

Before Tooth could reach him, Pitch sent a
huge Nightmare toward her. Tooth shrank back,
and Baby Tooth took cover in Jack's jacket.

"Whoa!" Pitch said to the Nightmare. "Easy
girl. Easy." He twirled his fingers through the
Nightmare's mane. He held some of the black sand
in his hand and then turned to Sandy.

"Look familiar, Sandman?" Pitch asked. "Took
me a while to perfect this little trick. Turning
dreams into Nightmares."

The Guardians all gasped.

Pitch chuckled. "Don't be nervous, it only riles
them up. They smell fear, you know."

"What fear?" Bunny asked. "Of *you*? No one's
been afraid of you since the Dark Ages."

Pitch's eyes flashed for just a moment, and Jack could see that Pitch lived to scare others. But then he managed a smile. "The Dark Ages," he said as he began to reminisce. "Everyone frightened. Miserable. Such happy times for me. Oh, the power I yielded.

"But then you showed up!" he continued. "With your wonder and light! Lifting their hearts and giving them hope!"

He explained to the Guardians, "Meanwhile, everyone wrote me off as just a bad dream. 'Oh, there's nothing to be afraid of. There's no such thing as the Boogeyman.' Well, that's all about to change."

A cracking sound filled the room. All the Guardians turned to see a beautiful column crumble.

"Oh, look." Pitch clapped his hands. "It's already happening."

"What is?" Jack asked.

"Children are waking up and realizing the Tooth Fairy never came," Pitch said. "Such a little thing, but to a child . . ."

"What's going on?" Jack cringed as more

columns fell and the palace broke apart.

"They don't believe in me anymore," Tooth explained sadly.

"Didn't they tell you, Jack?" Pitch asked. "It's great being a Guardian, but there's a catch. If enough kids stop believing, all their palaces and powers go away. And little by little, so do they."

Jack's jaw dropped as he began to understand.

Pitch nodded. "No Christmas or Easter or little fairies that come in the night. There will be nothing but fear and darkness and me! It's your turn not to be believed in!"

Bunny began to throw his boomerangs at Pitch. But Pitch escaped, flying through the palace on the back of Onyx, his favorite Nightmare.

The Guardians followed him. Jack brought up the rear.

Using eggs that were bombs, Bunny tried to slow Pitch down, but the eggs exploded in empty space.

"He's gone," North said, staring at the place where Pitch had disappeared.

Jack Frost can turn water to ice with just a touch of his magical staff, but he wishes he knew more about who he is and where he came from.

A dark presence
has returned.

North sounds the call and
gathers the Guardians to his
fortress at the North Pole.

The Guardians
are on their way!

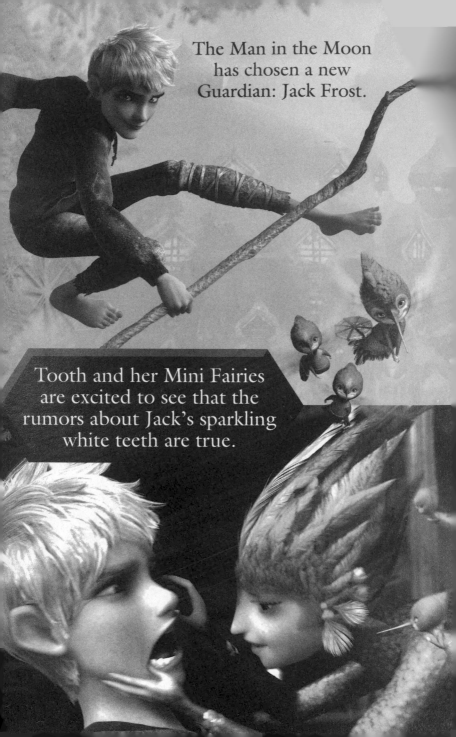

The Man in the Moon has chosen a new Guardian: Jack Frost.

Tooth and her Mini Fairies are excited to see that the rumors about Jack's sparkling white teeth are true.

But Jack doesn't want to
be a Guardian.

North asks Jack who he is.
What is Jack's center?

North shows Jack what's
at his center: eyes that
have always seen the
wonder in everything.

There's trouble at the Tooth Palace.
The Guardians climb into North's
sleigh. Everyone loves the sleigh . . .
everyone except Bunny!

And they're off!

Tooth stores every child's baby teeth at the Tooth Palace. The teeth hold the most important memories of childhood.

Now Pitch has taken the teeth!

The Guardians must get the teeth back and
stop Pitch before it's too late, and they need
Jack Frost's help. Will he join them?

Tooth sat down. She held an empty tooth box. Baby Tooth rested on a broken box nearby.

Jack walked over to them and then crouched low beside Tooth.

Bunny told North, "Okay, all right, I admit it. You were right about Pitch."

"This is one time I wish I was wrong," North replied. "But he will pay."

"I'm sorry about the fairies," Jack told Tooth.

Tooth sighed. "You should have seen them. They put up such a fight."

"Why would Pitch take the teeth?" Jack asked.

"It's not the teeth he wanted," Tooth explained. "It's the memories inside them."

Jack stared at her. "What do you mean?"

Tooth led Jack across the palace lagoon. The

water under his feet hardened into ice with each step.

"That's why we collect the teeth, Jack. They hold the most important memories of childhood." Tooth showed him a wall mural. It was a picture of memories being gathered. "My fairies and I watch over them, and when someone needs to remember what's important, we help them. We had every-one's here," she said. "Yours too."

"My memories?" Jack asked.

"From when you were young," Tooth answered. "Before you became Jack Frost."

Jack shook his head. "But I wasn't anyone before I was Jack Frost."

"Of course you were. We were all someone before we were chosen," Tooth said.

"What?" Jack didn't fully understand.

North entered the conversation. "You should have seen Bunny." He chuckled.

"Hey, I told you never to mention that!" Bunny said.

Jack was struggling with this new informa-tion. "That night at the Pond . . . I just . . . why, I assumed. Are you saying . . . Are you saying I had a life before that? With a home? And a family?"

"You really don't remember?" Tooth asked.

Jack's face was blank. "All these years, and the answers were right here." He looked around the crumbling palace. "If I find my memories, then I'll know why I'm here."

The wind lifted Jack off the lagoon. He was ready to follow Tooth to *his* storage drawer. Jack said, "You have to show me."

"I can't, Jack," Tooth said. "Pitch has them."

"Then we have to get them back!" Jack looked over his shoulder at the ancient mural. It began to disintegrate.

"Oh no. The children!" Tooth cried. "We're losing them. We're too late."

"No! No! No such thing as too late," North said. "Wait. Idea! Ha!" North knew how the Guardians could help. "We will collect the teeth."

"What?" Tooth asked.

"We get teeth! Children keep believing in *you*!" North declared.

"We're talking seven continents," Tooth said. "Millions of kids."

"Give me a break!" North told her. "You know

how many toys I deliver in one night?"

"And eggs I hide in one day?" Bunny put in.

North turned to Jack. "And, Jack, if you help us, we will get your memories."

Jack looked to Tooth, who agreed to the deal. Sandy gave Jack a thumbs-up. Bunny just groaned. Jack turned back to North and smiled.

In Shanghai, China, North shot out of a chimney and raced across the rooftop. "Quickly! Quickly!" he said as Bunny popped up a roof away.

"Here we go, here we go," Bunny chanted.

Jack zipped past Bunny. "Hop to it, rabbit. I'm five teeth ahead!"

"Yeah, right," Bunny replied. "Look, I'd tell you to stay outta my way, but, really, what's the point? Because you won't be able to keep up, anyway!"

"Is that a challenge, cottontail?" Jack asked.

"Oh, you don't wanna race a rabbit, mate," Bunny said.

"A race?" North asked Jack and Bunny. "Is it a race? It's going to be epic!"

Tooth darted around with Baby Tooth struggling to keep up. "Four bicuspids over there!" She pointed left. "An incisor two blocks east! Is that a molar? THEY'RE EVERYWHERE!" Tooth was overwhelmed by the task in this city alone. She flitted off the rooftop and straight into a billboard advertising toothpaste. "Ow," she said, moaning and rubbing her head.

Jack leaped to the top of the billboard to check on her. "You okay?"

"Fine," Tooth said. "Sorry. It's been a really long time since I've been out in the field."

"How long is a long time?" Jack asked.

"Four hundred and forty years," she replied. "Give or take."

Before Jack could respond, Tooth noticed a tiny glow under the pillow of a little girl in a nearby room. And without another word, Tooth rushed off.

Inside a dimly lit bedroom, Jack was about to snag a tooth when Bunny popped out of a hole in the floor. Bunny grabbed the tooth and then got away.

In the next city, North discovered two teeth under a pillow. He nabbed both. "Yipa!" he said triumphantly as he hurried off.

At another home, Bunny got several teeth from a sleeping child. "Jackpot!" He glanced around the room. There were hockey posters on the walls, and the shelves were loaded with trophies. "Looks like you're a bit of a brumby, hey mate," Bunny remarked.

North stood by a boy's bed. "It's a piece of pie!" he said softly. But as he reached forward, Bunny came up through a rabbit hole in the floor. While the two Guardians competed for the tooth, Sandy slipped between them and took the prize for himself.

"That's my tooth!" North whisper-yelled at the Sandman's back. "Sandy! Sandy!"

Bunny continued on his mission to sabotage Jack. When Jack came into the next room, Bunny opened a rabbit hole and Jack fell through. Bunny took the tooth and then disappeared down another rabbit hole.

Tooth reached under a child's pillow and pulled out a tooth. The tooth was perfect, but there was a mouse attached to the root. Baby Tooth immediately tackled the mouse, shaking him free.

"Whoa, whoa, whoa!" Tooth pulled Baby Tooth back. "Take it easy there, champ. He's one of us. Part of the European division." Tooth turned to the mouse and then asked if he was okay in French, *"Ça va?"*

In yet another city Bunny was about to grab his next tooth, but when he reached under the child's pillow, he found a note instead. The note showed an arrow pointing toward the window. Bunny followed the direction of the arrow. There he found North, holding the kid's tooth and grinning.

"Huh?" Bunny said in surprise as North dashed toward another house.

Bunny was certain the next tooth was his, but when he reached the roof, he heard the cracking sound of ice and frost. "Crikey!" Bunny began to slip. Tumbling down the slick, tilted roof, Bunny passed Jack. Jack easily reached out and snagged the tooth from Bunny.

"Yes!" Jack cheered, but an instant later a stream of dreamsand surrounded Jack.

Sandy waved good-bye as he snagged the tooth for himself.

North dropped down a chimney into a cottage. He was excited to get this tooth and increase his count. As he touched down on the wooden logs in the fireplace, a fuzzy paw reached out. "Ha-ha! Ho, ho, ho!" Bunny laughed and lit the fire.

"Ahh!" North screamed, bursting out of the hot and blazing chimney to the cool safety of the roof.

North, Sandy, Jack, and Bunny met up on a rooftop. The competition had been good fun, and they each had a large sack filled with teeth.

"Wow!" Tooth was impressed. "You guys collect teeth and leave gifts as fast as my fairies."

The Guardians stared at one another.

Tooth surveyed their panicked looks and asked, "You guys have been leaving gifts, right?"

They were all too embarrassed to reply.

A few minutes later the faithful Guardians stood in line at a coin dispenser. They each took a turn stuffing wrinkled bills into the slot, changing cash into coins.

Then they got back to work.

North took a tooth and then put a coin and a candy cane in its place.

Bunny carried coins in his thick, fuzzy paws. He left a coin and a pair of Easter eggs on a child's bed.

Baby Tooth stuffed a heavy coin beneath a feather pillow.

Tooth left a coin for a sleeping child.

Sandy entered a house through the doggy door and then left a kid a coin.

A toddler spotted the Guardians through his bedroom window, jumping from roof to roof. He was so surprised, he dropped his cup of juice.

Finally the Guardians climbed back into the sleigh. Nearby, a Nightmare spy watched North take up the reins. As the Guardians lifted off into the sky, the Nightmare vaporized down a street drain, slipping into the sewer.

Pitch was inside his darkened lair, standing near a light-covered Globe, exactly like the one in North's Workshop. Hanging on the walls around his head were the stolen boxes of teeth. The teeth glittered in the Globe's light while Mini Fairies stared out, trapped in cages.

Pitch poked a finger at his Globe. He turned to the Nightmare that was slithering into the room. "Why aren't the lights going out?"

The Nightmare let out a soft whinny.

Pitch stamped his foot angrily. If the lights weren't going out on his Globe, it meant that children still believed. His voice boomed. "They're collecting the teeth?"

The Mini Fairies began twittering at the news. Their hopeful, tiny, voices echoed throughout the Lair.

Pitch swirled to face them. "Oh, pipe down," he demanded. "Or I'll stuff a pillow with you." Scowling, Pitch raised a hand and formed an image of Sandy in nightmare sand. "Fine, have your last hurrah. For tomorrow, all your pathetic scrambling will be for nothing."

Pitch crushed Sandy's image with his fist.

CHAPTER
SEVEN

Jamie's awesome toy robot stood watch on his bedside table. As he slept, Jamie's tongue rested in the new gap between his teeth.

Tooth fluttered over Jamie's head while Jack stood by the bed.

"Left central incisor, knocked out in a freak sledding accident." Tooth raised her eyes to meet Jack's. "I wonder how that could have happened, Jack?"

Jack laughed, looking at the picture Jamie had drawn and hung on his wall. The one of Jamie on his sled, midair, pelting his friends with snowballs.

Jack blushed. "Kids, huh?"

Tooth smiled at the peacefully dreaming boy. "This was always the part I liked most—seeing the kids." Tooth paused before adding, "Why did I ever stop doing this?"

Jack could see how much Tooth loved her job. "It's a little different up close, huh?" Jack remarked.

Tooth nodded. "Thanks for being here, Jack. I wish I had known about your memory. I could've helped you."

"Yeah, well, look, let's just get you taken care of," Jack said. "Then it's Pitch's turn."

A sudden noise outside attracted their attention. Tooth and Jack both turned to the window.

"Here you are!" North was hauling a large sack over his shoulder. The windowsill groaned as North squeezed himself through. Sandy and Baby Tooth came in after.

"What gives, slowpokes?" North asked.

"SHHHHH," Tooth whispered a warning. Jamie was still asleep.

"How you feeling, Toothy?" North asked softly.

"Believed in," Tooth replied.

"Ha-ha!" North gave a little chuckle. "That's what I wanted to hear."

"Oh, I see how it is. . . ." Bunny arrived through

his rabbit hole. "All working together to make sure the rabbit gets last place."

North held his finger up to his lips. "Shhhhhh."

Jack raised his bulging bag of teeth. "You think I need help to beat a bunny? Check it out, Peter Cottontail."

"You call that a bag of choppers?" Bunny's bag was even bigger. "Now *that's* a bag of choppers."

"Gentlemen! Gentlemen!" North interrupted. "This is about Tooth. It's not a competition! But if it was"—his bag was the largest of them all—"I win. YEEEEHAAAAAW!" North danced around Jamie's room in a Russian jig.

Suddenly a bright light caught North in the belly.

"Oh no." He stopped dancing.

"Santa Claus?" Jamie asked, rubbing his eyes. He sat up, holding a flashlight and peering around the room. "The Easter Bunny? Sandman? The Tooth Fairy?" Jamie popped up from his pillows. "I knew you'd come!"

"Surprise!" Tooth said, pretending that this was all very normal. "We came."

"He can see us?" Jack asked.

Jamie scanned the room, completely amazed.

He looked at everyone except Jack, whom he still couldn't see.

"Most of us," Bunny replied.

"Shhh," Tooth warned. "You guys, he's still awake."

"Sandy, knock him out," Bunny suggested.

"Huh?" Jamie scooted back on the bed.

"With the dreamsand, ya gumbies." Bunny shook his head.

With that, Jamie's dog woke up, yawned, and sniffed the air toward Bunny.

"No." Jamie told the dog. "Stop! That's the Easter Bunny. What are you doing? Down!"

The dog came nose-to-nose with Bunny.

"All right," Bunny said. "Nobody panic."

Jack thought it was funny. "But that's a greyhound. Do you know what greyhounds *do* to rabbits?"

"I think it's a pretty safe bet he's never met a rabbit like me," Bunny said.

Sandy made a baseball out of dreamsand as Jack rolled his eyes at Bunny. Jack noticed an alarm clock on the bedside table.

Bunny continued, "Six foot one, nerves of steel,

master of Tai Chi, and the ancient art of—"

Jack couldn't help himself. He reached over and pressed a button on the alarm clock with his staff. *RINNGG!*

"Crikey!" Bunny exclaimed as the dog leaped toward him. He hopped around the room, the greyhound nipping at his tail.

"Stop! Sit!" Jamie commanded. "Down, girl, down!"

The dog chased Bunny over the bed and up the walls while Tooth struggled to silence the alarm clock.

"Sandy!" cried North, urging him to throw the ball at the dog and end this madness.

But before Sandy could throw it, the dog knocked into him. Dreamsand went flying.

Tooth shook her head at the chaos. "This is not proper Tooth Fairy behavior," she scolded.

North ducked when the dreamsand sailed toward him, causing the dreamsand baseball to smack Tooth directly in the face. The sleepy dust knocked her and Baby Tooth out cold. They both fell to the floor with a thud. A dreamy little tooth floated above each fairy's head.

Streams of dreamsand filled Jamie's bedroom.

Bunny dodged the dog, saying, "This thing's rabid! Get this dingo off me!" He caught a whiff of sand. "Oh no." Bunny yawned before falling asleep, dreaming of carrots.

Next to him, the dog toppled over and began to dream of bunnies.

"Candy canes," North said before he also began to snooze. Unfortunately, when North fell asleep, he was still standing up. As his dreams took over, North hit Jamie's mattress before hitting the floor, springing Jamie into the air like a catapult.

"Whoaaaa!" Jamie shrieked before Sandy caught him. Sandy dumped a bit of dreamsand on the boy's head, then put him back into bed.

"Whoops." Jack took a long look around the now-quiet room. Tooth and Baby Tooth were snoozing in a corner while Bunny was snuggling with North.

"Oh, I really wish I had a camera right now," Jack said.

At that moment, Sandy spotted something dark and shadowy outside the window.

Jack turned to see where Sandy was looking.

"Sandy, c'mon," Jack said. "We can find Pitch."

Sandy paused to look at everyone sleeping soundly in Jamie's room, then followed Jack out into the night.

Sophie toddled into her big brother's room while everyone was sleeping. She giggled as she reached into North's pocket and took out his magical snow globe.

"Pretty!" Sophie said. She carried the globe over to Bunny. "Easter Bunny!" Sophie said joyfully. "Hop! Hop! Hop!"

Imitating a bunny's bounce, Sophie shook the globe. It revealed a beautiful image of Bunny's Warren. Delighted, Sophie began to take the globe back to her room, but on the way, she tripped. The globe smashed onto the floor, and with a flash of light, a magical portal opened in front of her.

A warm breeze came from the portal, and Sophie leaned forward to check it out.

"Whuh-huh?" North woke up an instant too late. By the time North opened his eyes, Sophie was already gone.

Jack and Sandy followed two Nightmares across the rooftops of Burgess.

"Wahooo!" Jack said, riding the wind to catch one of the Nightmares. The Nightmare flew over a rooftop. Jack followed it.

Jack chased the Nightmare away from a house, just in time to see Sandy wrestling with the other one. The Nightmare was strong, but Sandy was stronger. With a blast, Sandy changed the dark grit into golden dreamsand and then rode the dream, now shaped like a stingray, through the town.

Jack went after the one that got away. "Haaaa!" he shouted as the Nightmare turned down an alley and then traveled up to another rooftop. "I got it!" Jack blasted frost from his staff, freezing the Nightmare into a solid mass.

"Sandy!" Jack called. "Sandy, did you see that? Look at this thing." He poked the Nightmare with his staff.

But it wasn't Sandy who appeared behind him.

"Frost?" Pitch was standing on the same roof as Jack.

Jack shot a streak of frost at him, but Pitch dodged it.

"You know," Pitch said, "for a 'neutral party,' you spend an awful lot of time with those weirdos. This isn't your fight, Jack."

Jack raised his staff. "You made it my fight when you stole those teeth."

Pitch squinted. "Teeth? Why do you care about the teeth?" A noise behind Pitch caused him to turn. Sandy was standing there. Pitch quickly moved away. "Now this is who I'm looking for—" Before Pitch could finish the sentence, Sandy blasted him with dreamsand.

Pitch ducked. He aimed his nightmare sand at Sandy. Jack ducked as Sandy was forced onto a high ledge.

Sandy nearly fell backward, but saved himself at the last minute. Using a wave of dreamsand, Sandy shot back at Pitch, snaring him in dreamsand and throwing him off the roof, causing him to crash onto the street below.

Jack peered down at Pitch. "Remind me not to get on your bad side," he told Sandy.

Pitch shook off the crash, stepping away as

Sandy and Jack flew off the roof and into the street.

"Okay, easy. You can't blame me for trying, Sandy. You don't know what it's like to be weak and hated. It was stupid of me to mess with your dreams. So I'll tell you what: You can have 'em back," Pitch offered.

Before Sandy and Jack could react, hundreds of Nightmares filled the street and stood on the surrounding rooftops.

Jack turned to Sandy. "You take the ones on the left. I'll take the ones on the right."

Pitch rose from the ground, riding his Nightmare horse, Onyx. "Boo!" Pitch shouted at Sandy and Jack. The Nightmares began to charge.

Jack and Sandy huddled together, back-to-back, searching for an escape.

Suddenly the sound of sleigh bells and reindeer hooves filled the air.

North's sleigh zoomed overhead, buzzing past Pitch and his Nightmares.

Bunny had been asleep in the sleigh, but finally woke up. He was a bit confused when he said, "Get out of my Warren." Then realizing where he was, Bunny gathered his boomerangs for battle.

Sandy flung dreamsand at the Nightmares. Jack used his staff to fight them off one by one.

Tooth and Baby Tooth flew out of the sleigh, coming to Jack's and Sandy's aid.

While Jack knocked Nightmares away with his staff, Tooth used her wings to slice through them.

Like a general at war, Pitch commanded his Army of Nightmares to continue the attack.

Bunny jumped from the sleigh onto a roof. His boomerangs flew, dissolving every Nightmare in their paths. When the sleigh passed by, Bunny hopped back in.

"Ha, ha, ha," North cheered. "Come on!"

Jack dodged two Nightmares, but a third one knocked the staff out of his hand. Slipping from the rooftop, Jack began to fall.

"Aaaaaaah!" He got control by grabbing back his staff and hooking it to the sleigh's rails.

"You might want to duck," Bunny told Jack as he flung a boomerang at one of the Nightmares.

Pitch's Nightmares surrounded Sandy, and he valiantly fought them off with pleasant dreams of his own.

"We gotta help Sandy!" Jack pointed from the sleigh.

"Hyah!" North flicked the reins.

But before they could reach Sandy, Pitch formed nightmare sand into a bow and arrow. He aimed at Sandy's back. The arrow hit Sandy between the shoulders and then exploded.

"Noooo!" Jack yelled.

Jack leaped out of the sleigh.

"Jack!" North called after him.

Pitch chuckled as the Nightmares took over Sandy's dreams.

"Ha, ha, ha, ha, ha! Don't fight the fear, little man," Pitch said.

North pulled the sleigh around for a rescue mission, but Nightmares surrounded him. "Hurry, hurry," North called to Jack, who was on his way to help Sandy.

Sandy's dreamsand was turning black as the bad dreams took over. "I'd say sweet dreams, but there aren't any left," Pitch said.

Jack continued on, fighting off Nightmares, struggling to reach Sandy.

"Sandy," North said, moaning. A few seconds later, Sandy's dreamsand was entirely black.

Sandy was gone.

Pitch clapped his hands with joy.

"No . . . NOOOOO!" Jack reached Pitch and then rushed forward, his staff bright with energy that would soon be dispensed at Pitch.

Pitch turned and directed his Nightmares at Jack.

It was too much to take at once. The Nightmares surrounded Jack and began to overtake him.

Pitch stood back, smiling.

Jack swung his staff and then rode a gust of wind out of the Nightmare cloud. Frost and ice filled the street. The attacking Nightmares turned into snow.

"Aaahh!" Pitch was caught by surprise. He was tossed back out of the street and far, far away.

The effort took all Jack's energy. He collapsed. North's sleigh finally reached the rooftop.

Tooth quickly picked up Jack and carried him to safety.

"Jack, how did you do that?" she asked.

"I didn't know I could," Jack replied groggily.

As the sleigh zipped off into the night, Pitch stood up and looked around at where he'd crash-landed. At first he was angry, but then he was pleased.

Smiling, he watched the sleigh slip into a snow globe portal.

Jack Frost was a worthy opponent.

"Finally!" Pitch dusted himself off. "Someone who knows how to have a little fun!" He waved at Jack as the sleigh took off to the North Pole. Pitch was looking forward to the next time they met.

Back in the Globe Room at the North Pole, the Guardians held a ceremony for Sandy. Candles surrounded his empty spot on the floor.

Tooth, North, and Bunny held hands while bells echoed throughout the room.

Jack used his finger to draw a picture of Sandy on a frosted window and then sighed.

North walked over to Jack. "Are you all right?" he asked.

"I just wish I could've done something," Jack replied.

"Done something?" North asked. "Jack, you stood up to Pitch. You saved us."

Jack pinched his lips together. "But Sandy wo—"

North interrupted. "Would be proud of what you did."

Jack sighed again, nodding.

"I don't know what you were in your past life, but in *this* life you are a Guardian." North touched Jack's shoulder.

"But how can I know who I am until I know who I was?" asked Jack.

"You will," North assured him. "I feel it in my belly."

Jack allowed North to lead him back toward the Globe of Belief.

"Look how fast they're going out." Tooth pointed at the tiny lights across the continents.

"It's fear," Jack said, leaning in closer to the Globe. "He's tipped the balance."

Bunny wasn't going to let all the lights disappear. "Hey, buck up, ya sad sacks! We can still turn this around! Easter's tomorrow! I need your help. I say we pull out all the stops, and we get those little lights flickering again!"

Energized, North led everyone to the toy factory. "Bunny is right. As much as it pains me to say, old friend, this time Easter *is* more important than Christmas!"

"Hey! Did everyone hear that?" asked Bunny.

"We must hurry to the Warren," said North. "Everyone, to the sleigh!"

"Oh no, mate," Bunny said. "My Warren, my rules. Buckle up." With a heavy tap on the floor, Bunny opened a rabbit hole, and the entire group fell into the floor.

"Shostakovich!" cried North.

The Guardians, Jack, plus two yetis and a few elves landed just outside the entrance to the Warren.

Due to their sizes, North and the yetis landed hard, but that didn't dampen North's good mood. "Buckle up," he said, chuckling to himself. "That's very funny."

But Bunny was all business. He stood on a moss-covered rock. It began to rise. Below the moss it wasn't a rock but an egg made of stone; one of Bunny's Sentinel eggs that guarded the Warren. "Now, listen. Down here the eggs are safe. Up top, they'll be well hidden," he told his guests as he hopped on other Sentinel eggs that had begun to rise out of the ground. "It is our job to protect them in the tunnels on the way to the big show. If we get that far, we've got ourselves Easter."

As he entered Bunny's home, Jack couldn't believe his eyes. The Warren was a gorgeous, lush, green meadow, with rocks and streams and colorful flowers.

Suddenly, Bunny raised his ears and sniffed the air. Something was wrong.

A faint shout came from one of Bunny's egg tunnels. Little eggs were rushing out of the passageway.

North drew his sword, Bunny took out his boomerang, and Jack held tightly to his staff. The Guardians were expecting Pitch, but then Jamie's sister, Sophie, popped out of the tunnel. She laid eyes on one of the elves and began to run after him.

"What is SHE doing HERE?" Bunny asked, horrified.

North felt around in his coat to discover his pocket was empty. "Snow globe?"

"Crickey!" exclaimed Bunny. "Somebody do something!"

"Don't look at me," said Jack. "I'm invisible, remember?"

At this point, Sophie had managed to catch the elf, and was dragging him through the green grass by the bell on the top of his hat.

"Don't worry, Bunny. I bet she's a fairy fan," Tooth said as she flew to the delighted girl. "It's okay, little one."

"Pretty," Sophie said to Tooth.

"Awww." Tooth blushed. "You know what, I got something for you. Here it is." She pulled out a handful of teeth. "Look at all the pretty teeth with a little blood and gum on them."

Sophie screamed in Tooth's ear and then ran away.

Jack shook his head. "Blood and gums? When was the last time you guys actually hung out with kids?"

Tooth shrugged.

But Sophie got over her scare quickly, and soon she poked her head into a small tunnel and said, "Peekaboo."

"We are very busy bringing joy to children," North said. "We don't have time for . . . children." Embarrassed, he looked away.

Jack formed a snowflake in his hand. He blew a little wind behind it, and the flake floated toward Sophie. When she tried to grab it, Jack made a little more wind and began a game of chase.

"If one little kid can ruin Easter," Jack said, "then we're in worse shape than I thought."

Jack blew the snowflake toward Bunny while Sophie followed it, shouting, "Wheeee! Wheee, wheee, wheee!"

The flake landed on Bunny's nose.

Looking down at the little girl, Bunny finally smiled. "You wanna paint some eggs?"

"Okay!" Sophie answered brightly.

"Come on, then!" said Bunny.

At that moment, North looked around to see thousands and thousands of white eggs, all of which still needed to be decorated. "That's a lot of eggs!"

"Uh, how much time do we have?" asked Jack.

But Bunny was busy having fun. "Whoooo-hoooo!" He hopped along the meadow with Sophie on his back.

"Wheeee!" Sophie squealed with delight.

Everywhere Bunny stepped, flowers bloomed

beside his feet, white eggs turned to color, and the valley glittered like a rainbow.

"All right, troops, it's time to push back," Bunny commanded. "That means eggs everywhere! Heaps of you in every high-rise, farmhouse, and trailer park! In tennis shoes and cereal bowls. There will be bathtubs filled with my beautiful googies!"

And with that, the Guardians and the eggs got going on the preparations for Easter. The eggs marched single file into a multicolored stream. One of North's elves stood at the edge of a cliff. He couldn't get away fast enough as the eggs rushed toward him, and they all splashed down into the colored stream below to be painted and decorated for their big show at Easter tomorrow. The eggs emerged from the stream in every color and pattern imaginable (as did the unlucky elf).

A stray egg wandered off the path and ended up in a whirlpool. North fished it out, turning it around in the sunlight. The egg had a strange spiral pattern on it.

"Okay," North said. "That's a little strange."

"Naw, mate." Bunny carefully took the egg in his paw. "That's adorable."

Sophie led the colored eggs as they marched around Bunny. "There will be springtime!" Bunny encouraged. "On every continent! And I'm bringing hope with me."

Meanwhile, the yetis sprinkled glitter on some eggs, which then hopped down into different tunnels to be decorated with stripes.

Another yeti was hand painting some eggs when Bunny walked by. "Too Christmassy, mate. Paint 'em blue," he instructed.

Sophie and Bunny began to play again.

"What's that over there?" Bunny asked her.

Sophie searched through the grass and found a decorated egg. She showed it to Bunny. "That's a beauty!" Bunny exclaimed.

"Pretty," Sophie agreed.

Soon all the eggs were ready, decorated, and gathered at the tunnels, ready for their big moment up top.

"Not bad," Jack said, approving of the operation.

"Not bad yourself," Bunny replied.

"Look," Jack began, "I'm sorry about that whole kangaroo thing."

"It's the accent, isn't it?" Bunny asked him.

North and Tooth came to join Bunny and Jack. They all turned to see Sophie fast asleep.

"Ah, poor little ankle biter. Look at her, all tuckered out," Bunny said.

"I love her," said Tooth. "But I think it's time to get her home."

"How about I take her home?" Jack suggested.

Tooth looked concerned. "Jack, no! Pitch is—"

Jack cut her off. "No match for this," he said, showing off his staff. "Trust me. I'll be quick as a bunny."

Back in Burgess, Jack laid Sophie down into her bed. Baby Tooth had come with him to help with Sophie. When Sophie finally let go of him, she rolled over and then fell off the side of her mattress and onto the floor.

"Sophie?" her mother called from the hallway. "Is that you?"

Jack placed a blanket over Sophie and then left her comfortably snoozing on the rug.

Jack and Baby Tooth climbed out the window.

"We should get back," Jack started, when suddenly a voice called out.

"Jack!" It was a memory calling. Loud and clear. Jack looked to the forest near Jamie's house and felt the memory tug at him.

"Jack."

Jack took off toward the sound. Baby Tooth went with him.

"Jack."

Following the voice, Jack sprinted through the trees until he reached a clearing. In the center of the meadow was a child's old bed. It was broken and rotted.

Baby Tooth shivered, then pulled on Jack's jacket to try to drag him out of the forest.

"Don't worry," Jack tried to assure her. "There's still time."

With that, Jack whacked the bed with his staff. It broke away to reveal a dark, deep hole in the ground. The voice called Jack's name once again. With a shrug, Jack jumped in. Baby Tooth stayed close behind.

Jack and Baby Tooth followed the tunnels into a huge underground cavern. Every step of the way, Baby Tooth tugged on Jack's jacket, trying to get him to come back with her.

"Baby Tooth, come on! I have to find out what that is," Jack explained.

As they ventured farther, Jack realized they were in Pitch's Lair. Tooth's Mini Fairies were trapped in tiny cages, chirping and begging for Jack to rescue them. Along the walls, the boxes of stolen teeth were stacked like pirate treasure. Heaps of teeth were piled up in the center of the room.

"Shhh!" Jack told the little fairies. "Keep it down." He picked up a cage. "I'm gonna get you out of here, just as soon as I—"

The voice from his memory cut into his thoughts. "Jack . . . Jack . . ."

He shook his head to clear it. "As I can."

"Jack . . ."

The voice seemed to be coming from one of the closest mounds of baby teeth. Jack dropped to his knees, searching through the pile, ignoring the insistent chirping of the Mini Fairies and Baby Tooth's frantic tugs at his jacket. Jack just had to find the baby teeth that held the keys to his lost memories.

The room began to darken. Jack raised his head and discovered Pitch's shadow hovering above him.

"Looking for something?" Pitch asked. His shadow moved around the walls, then disappeared into a narrow, cramped hallway.

Pitch cackled with laughter as Jack raised his staff and began to follow.

"Don't be afraid, Jack," Pitch said. "I'm not going to hurt you."

"Afraid?" Jack continued searching for Pitch. "I'm not afraid of you."

"Maybe not," Pitch said. "But you *are* afraid of something."

"You think so, huh?" Jack asked.

Pitch's shadow then moved to a bridge above Jack's head. Shadows fell everywhere.

"I *know* so. It's the one thing I *always* know." Pitch stepped into the light and faced Jack. "People's greatest fears. Yours is that no one will ever believe in you."

Jack felt a surge of panic. He'd never told anyone what he was most afraid of, but somehow Pitch knew. Jack searched the room for a way out. He had to escape. The shadows in the cave surrounded him and what he thought was a wall was actually the floor. Jack spun around, desperate to find an exit.

Pitch had disappeared again, but his voice still boomed throughout the Lair. "And worst of all, you're afraid you'll never know *why*. Why *you*? Why were you chosen to be like this?"

At that moment, Jack found an exit, but it was closed off with bricks. He watched as Pitch's shadow moved in closer.

"Well, fear not, for the answer to that is right here." Pitch held out a tooth box toward Jack. The box had a picture of a little boy and the name JACK FROST written on it. "Do you want them, Jack?

Your memories?" Pitch jiggled the box so that the teeth rattled.

Jack held back his hands. He wanted to reach out and grab the teeth, but then again, he couldn't. Taking them from Pitch would be a mistake. While he debated what to do, Pitch moved back into the main area of the cavernous lair.

"Everything you wanted to know is in this little box," Pitch taunted.

Jack pursued Pitch, but every time he got close, Pitch moved away. It was as though Jack was trapped in a carnival fun house. More and more shadows of Pitch began to appear.

"Why did you end up like this?" the many Pitches continued. "Unseen. Unable to reach out to anyone. You want the answers so badly. You want to grab them and fly off with them, but you're afraid of what the Guardians will think."

Jack felt the shadows all around him. He was trapped in a corner.

"You're afraid of disappointing them," the many Pitches went on. "Well, let me ease your mind about one thing: They'll never accept you. Not *really*."

Jack waved his hands at the shadows. "Stop it!" he shouted. "Stop it!"

"After all, you're not one of them," Pitch said, pulling all the shadows of himself together and standing in front of Jack.

"You don't know what I am," Jack said, taking aim at Pitch with his staff.

Pitch laughed. "Of course I do. You're Jack Frost. You make a mess wherever you go. Why, you're doing it right now."

Pitch tossed Jack's tooth box into the air.

Jack caught it and then asked, "What did you do?"

Pitch smiled. "More to the point, Jack, what did *you* do?

With an echoing laugh, Pitch moved backward through the room. Anger filled Jack, and he lunged, but he wrapped his arms around nothing but air. An instant later Jack was swallowed into one of Pitch's blackest holes.

Jack landed in an egg tunnel and charged, ready to fight Pitch, but then he remembered he'd left someone behind . . . someone important. "Baby Tooth!" he cried out. When he tried to go back to Pitch's Lair, he ran right into one of Bunny's Sentinel eggs. His fingers closed around his tooth box in fear as he examined his surroundings. The eggs! Thousands of colored eggs were smashed in the tunnels surrounding the Warren.

"No . . . ," Jack said breathlessly.

Jack raced to find Bunny and the Guardians. Bunny was hiding in some bushes, watching an Easter egg hunt in England. The kids were wandering around a garden with disappointment in their eyes.

"Come on, let's go," one kid told the others. "There's nothing."

"Maybe he just hid them really well this year," suggested another kid.

Bunny hopped out and then scampered across the grass. "Kids! Oi!"

A boy gave up. "Nah, I checked everywhere," he reported. "There's nothing!"

"Yes, there is!" Bunny called out. "I mean, these aren't my best-lookin' googies, but they'll do in a pinch." Bunny held out a broken egg.

"I can't believe it," a girl said.

"I know." Bunny looked down sadly at his colored bits of shell.

"There's no such thing as the Easter Bunny," the girl told the others.

"What?" Bunny cleared his ears.

The children began to walk away from the park. Bunny chased them down, shouting, "No! Wrong! Not—not true. I'm right in front of ya, mate."

The kids passed through Bunny as if he were vapor, and continued down the path.

"Let's get out of here," a boy said.

Bunny touched his belly. Tugged at his ears. He was there. He knew he was there!

"They don't see me." Bunny's shoulders drooped. "They don't see me."

Jack arrived just as the kids were giving up their egg search. He hung back while Tooth went to comfort Bunny.

"Where were you, Jack?" North came up behind him. North looked exhausted. His red coat was stained and tattered. "The Nightmares attacked the tunnels. They smashed every egg, crushed every basket. Nothing made it to the surface."

Tooth came over to Jack and North. She spotted

the box in Jack's hands and then asked, "Where'd you get that?"

"I was . . . . It's . . ." Jack stumbled over his words.

Tooth was furious. "Where's Baby Tooth? Oh, Jack, what have you done?"

"That is why you weren't here?" North asked. "You were with Pitch instead?

"No, listen, listen . . . I'm sorry. I didn't mean for this to happen," Jack tried to explain.

Bunny hopped over. "He has to go," he said without hesitation.

Jack was stunned. "What?"

Bunny looked heartbroken as he said, "We should never have trusted you. Easter is new beginnings, new life. Easter is about hope." He groaned. "And now it's gone."

Jack turned from Bunny to look at Tooth and North. They both turned away from him. It was exactly as Pitch had warned. The Guardians didn't need him. They didn't want him around anymore.

Reaching into his pocket, Jack pulled out the little Russian doll North had given him in the

Workshop. He stared at it for a long moment, then tossed the doll to the ground. Jack created a big gust of wind and then leaped into the breeze.

Back in Burgess, it was already late afternoon, and Jamie stood on a ladder, still searching for Easter eggs in the rain gutters around his house. As he looked over the roof, the ladder began to topple.

"Whoaaa, whoa, whoa, aaaah!" Jamie shrieked when the ladder tipped over. He grabbed the gutter for support, but it broke loose, and Jamie crashed down into a mound of snow.

Rising, he dusted snow off his back. On second look, the Easter egg he thought he saw turned out to be a dirty old tennis ball. Jamie's friends began to laugh.

They picked up their empty Easter baskets.

"Let's check the park again," Jamie suggested.

Caleb was annoyed. "Really?"

"For what, the Easter Bunny?" Claude added.

"Guys, I told you," Jamie said. "I saw him! He's way bigger than I thought, and he's got these cool boomerang things—"

"Ah, man, seriously?" Claude rolled his eyes.

Jamie couldn't believe what he was hearing. "What's happened to you guys?"

"It was a dream," Caleb explained. "You should be happy you still get dreams like that and not—"

"Nightmares," Cupcake finished his sentence.

The others turned to walk away. Pippa held back. "Forget it, Jamie. There's no Easter this year."

Jamie stood alone, holding an empty Easter basket. "He really is real," he muttered to himself. "I know he is."

Up at the North Pole, the yetis stood watch at the Globe of Belief. Lights were going out faster than they could count.

After he left the Guardians, Jack went down to Antarctica. He stood on the edge of an iceberg, holding the tooth box. He wondered if he should just throw it out into the ocean.

Pitch came out of the shadows and stood next to Jack.

"I thought this might happen," Pitch remarked.

Jack didn't look up.

"You can't blame me, Jack," Pitch continued. "They're the ones who abandoned you. But I understand."

Now Jack turned to face Pitch, and he blasted frost at him. Pitch met the frost with nightmare sand.

"You don't understand anything!" Jack cried, continuing to hurl ice and frost at Pitch.

"No?" Pitch asked as he blocked all of Jack's attempts with nightmare sand. "I don't know what it's like to be cast out? To long for a family?"

Lowering his staff, Jack began to listen to what Pitch was saying.

"Oh, don't look so surprised. I was someone once too, you know." Pitch moved closer. "We don't have to be alone, Jack. I believe in you. And I know children will too."

Jack gave Pitch his full attention. "In me?" he asked.

"Yes!" Pitch answered, and gestured to the white frost and black sand covering the iceberg. "Look what we can do! What goes together better than cold and dark?"

Jack looked around at the frost and sand sculptures as Pitch continued. "We can make them believe," Pitch said. "We'll give them a world where everything is—"

"Pitch-black," Jack suggested, realizing then that this was all about Pitch's personal fame.

Pitch quickly added, "And Jack Frost too. They'll believe in *both* of us."

Jack considered the offer, then said, "No, they'll *fear* both of us. And that's not what I want." He turned to walk away. "Now, for the last time, leave me alone."

"Very well," Pitch said. "You want to be left alone? Done. But first . . ." A familiar, tinkly sound forced Jack to spin back around.

"Baby Tooth!" Jack charged forward to rescue her from Pitch.

"The staff, Jack," Pitch demanded. "You have a bad habit of interfering. Now hand it over, and I'll let her go."

Pitch tightened his grasp, and Baby Tooth squeaked.

She couldn't breathe.

Jack gave Pitch his staff.

Pitch scooped it up happily, twirling the magical staff in his hand.

"All right," Jack told Pitch. "Now let her go."

Pitch chuckled. "No. You said you wanted to be alone." Baby Tooth wriggled in Pitch's hand and pecked at it. Pitch cried out and threw Baby Tooth into the air. She fell into an ice canyon.

As Baby Tooth was falling through the air, Jack lunged, screaming, "No!"

Then Pitch took Jack's staff and broke it in half. Lightning exploded from the stick. Nightmares swirled around Jack, slamming him into a wall of ice. The iceberg began to crack. Jack stumbled forward, moaning softly as chunks of ice collapsed around him. Pitch threw the pieces of staff aside.

Unable to get sure footing, Jack tumbled into a large crack in the ice, down into an endless frozen chasm.

As he fell, Jack could hear Pitch's evil laughter echoing far, far above.

The crack in the ice was not endless. Jack landed hard at the bottom. Aching from the fall, Jack raised himself up and looked around. In an icy corner, he discovered Baby Tooth lying on the ground.

"Baby Tooth!" Jack held her gently in his hands. "You all right?"

Baby Tooth nodded, but she was cold and injured. Jack hugged her close. She shivered.

"Sorry, bad idea," he said, holding Baby Tooth away. "All I can do is keep you cold." He sighed. "Pitch was right, I make a mess out of everything."

Baby Tooth wriggled herself into Jack's jacket pocket, where it was warm . . . and where Jack had stashed his tooth box.

Too tired to even think about getting out, Jack leaned back against a wall and began to close his eyes. A voice called out to him from his memory.

"Jack . . . Jack . . ." He opened his eyes to discover a golden glow coming from the tooth box in his pocket. "Jack," the voice said again.

Baby Tooth gave him a look that meant he should open the box.

Jack reached out toward the lid, and as he did, the top popped open. Inside were a handful of his baby teeth. The teeth glowed with intense light.

Memories washed over Jack like a waterfall.

His family lived in colonial times, in the same small village Jack had come to when he first awoke in the moonlight. And it was the village that had grown into the town of Burgess, where Jamie lived today.

He heard his mother calling, "Come on, Jack. You can't have fun all the time." Then Jack saw himself as a child, playing in the trees.

"Stop tricking us," Jack's sister called playfully.

Another memory flooded Jack. He and his family were warming themselves by a big fire. He wore antlers, trying to make everyone laugh.

"You're funny, Jack," a boy said.

The memory changed again. Now young Jack was out at the Pond with his sister, ice-skating in the center of the frozen water. As a child, Jack had brown eyes and brown hair, not Jack Frost's blue eyes and white hair.

A small crack was forming in the ice under his sister's skates. She wobbled, and the crack began to grow.

"Jack, I'm scared," his sister said.

"I know, I know, but you're gonna be all right. You're not gonna fall in. We're gonna have a little fun instead." Jack looked around for the safest way back to solid ground.

"No, we're not," his sister replied.

"Would I trick you?" Jack asked.

She was so frightened, a tear rolled down her face. "Yes! You *always* play tricks!"

Jack giggled. "Well, all right. But not this time. I promise. I promise you're gonna be . . ." He paused to look at the ice cracks. "You're gonna be fine." Jack stared into his sister's eyes. "You have to believe in me."

His sister choked back her tears and gave a small smile.

Jack told her what to do. "You wanna play a game? We're going to play hopscotch! Like we play every day." He showed his sister how to make the first leap toward the Pond's edge.

"It's as easy as one . . ." Jack jumped, but landed unsteadily. Grinning, as if his stumble was on purpose, he called out, "Two." Jack leaped again. "Three!" He was at the shore.

He held out his arms toward his sister. "All right," he said. "Now it's your turn." Jack reached down by his feet and picked up a stick lying on the ice. He held out his new staff toward her. "One."

She hopped carefully.

"That's it, that's it," Jack said. He pushed the staff out, so she could grab it. "Two."

She was almost there.

"Three." Jack's sister grabbed the end of the staff, and using all his strength, Jack flung her to the shore. But he couldn't hold on to his own balance, and Jack was thrust back onto the Pond. He crashed through the ice, into the freezing cold water.

"Jack!" his sister shouted.

Jack looked up through the ice to make sure she was safe. And then he began to sink.

Under the water, Jack could see the full moon shining down on him. The moonlight grew brighter and brighter until Jack's entire body began to glow. His eyes flashed open.

They had changed from brown to blue.

Jack sat up and looked at Baby Tooth. "Did you see that?" he asked, excited about the memory.

Baby Tooth tweeted. She was excited for Jack,

but she couldn't see into his memory.

"It was me!" Jack pushed himself up to stand. "I had a family. I had a sister!" He slowed down as he realized just what his memories meant. "I saved her."

Suddenly, moonlight filled the narrow cavern at the bottom of the ice crack. Jack looked up to see the moon peeking out at him from behind a cloud.

"That's why you chose me," he whispered to the Man in the Moon. "I'm a Guardian."

The moon shone a little brighter.

Baby Tooth tried to flit out of Jack's hand, but she was too injured.

"We have to get out of here," Jack said as he saw his broken staff lying in two pieces on the ice.

Jack tried to put the staff back together, but it kept falling apart. Finally, Jack managed to throw off a blue spark, which turned to light. The wooden pieces melded together, and the staff became whole again.

Jack smiled. "Come on, Baby Tooth! I owe you one."

With Baby Tooth in his pocket, Jack rode the wind out of the cavern and straight to Pitch's Lair. Moving quickly, they set all the Mini Fairies free.

Once the cages were open, Jack told them, "Come on, let's go." But none of them moved.

"What's wrong?" Jack asked. "None of you can fly?"

Jack was struggling with how to help them when Baby Tooth drew his attention to Pitch's Globe. It was dark. It looked as though there were no lights left.

There were no longer any children who believed.

At the North Pole, a yeti was putting the last, freshly painted red robot on a shelf when the factory started to shake. All the robots fell off the shelf. The yeti groaned.

"Paint 'em black!" Pitch's voice boomed as nightmare sand began to streak around the factory.

The yetis and elves ran around the factory in fear, knocking into all the toys and prototypes.

In the Globe Room, black sand covered the Globe, and then Pitch materialized out of the sand.

"You're all free to go!" he announced. "We won't be needing any Christmas toys this year, thank you! Nor ever again! Look!"

Pitch could barely contain his glee as he and the yetis and the elves watched the remaining lights go out. It was just as he had planned!

Pitch waited for the final light to disappear. And waited. And waited.

"No," Pitch said to himself.

At the same moment that Pitch watched that one light, Jack saw it too.

"Jamie!" Jack cheered.

There was no time to lose. Jack was off to Jamie's house as fast as the wind could take him.

CHAPTER
TEN

Jamie was in his bed, talking to his old stuffed bunny rabbit.

"Okay, look, you and I are obviously at what they call a crossroads. So here's what's gonna happen—"

Jack appeared at Jamie's window and moved in closer to hear.

"If it wasn't a dream and if you are real, then you have to prove it. Like, right now." Jamie stared at the bunny. When nothing happened, Jamie said, "I believed in you for a long time, okay? Like, my whole life, in fact. So you kinda owe me now." Jamie hugged the rabbit to his chest. "You don't have to do much, just a little sign so I know. Anything. Anything at all." Moments passed in silence before Jamie dropped the toy to the floor.

"I knew it," he whispered.

Jack slipped through the window and into Jamie's room. He watched as Jamie's eyes grew dark. His faith was fading fast. Jack had to do something.

Blowing frost onto Jamie's window, Jack drew an Easter egg on the icy surface.

"Huh?" Jamie noticed the image. In a super-swoop, Jamie grabbed his stuffed rabbit back off the floor. "He's real!"

Jack drew a bunny in the frosted glass, then using his magic powers, he concentrated on getting the drawing to hop across the window.

"Whoa." Jamie was thrilled as the rabbit made of frost leaped into the bedroom and then burst into hundreds of snowflakes above his head.

"Snow?" Jamie asked.

A large flake landed on Jamie's nose. The snowflake glowed blue. Jamie took a long look, considering, then whispered, "Jack Frost?" When no one replied, he stood on the bed and shouted, "Jack Frost!"

"He said it again." Jack muttered as he came out of hiding. "He said . . . You said . . ."

Jamie turned. "Jack Frost."

"That's right!" Jack cheered. "But that's me! Jack Frost! That's my name! You said *my* name!"

Jamie stood there, jaw hanging open, eyes wide in shock.

"Wait." Jack realized something important. "Can you hear me?"

Jamie nodded.

"Can you *see* me?"

Jamie nodded.

"He sees me! He sees me!" Jack leaped with joy, and the room suddenly exploded with snow.

"You just made it snow," Jamie remarked.

"I know!" Jack let more flakes fly.

"In my room," Jamie said.

"I *know*!" Jack sang out.

"You're real?" Jamie asked.

"Yeah," Jack said. "Who do you think brings you all the blizzards and snow days, and you remember when you went flying on the sled the other day?"

Jamie glanced at the drawing he'd made, still taped to his wall. "That was you?"

"That was *me*!" Jack said.

"Cool," Jamie gushed.

"Right?" Jack agreed.

"But what about the Easter Bunny and the Tooth Fairy?" Jamie asked.

"Real, real, real!" Jack said. "Every one of us is real!"

Jamie clapped his hands. "I knew it!

Just then, Jamie's Mom called from down the hall. "Jamie, who are you talking to?"

"Um," Jamie said, grinning, "Jack Frost."

Jamie's Mom laughed. "Uh, okay."

The sound of thunder made Jack and Jamie turn to the window.

"Whoa, whoa, whoa." It was North and Tooth on the sleigh. The sleigh was out of control and crash-landed in Jamie's yard. The reindeer got loose and made a break for the woods.

"Come back!" North called to them.

"North! Are you okay?" Tooth asked.

"It's official," North replied. "My powers are kaput."

That's when Tooth noticed Jack rushing toward them. Tooth tried to fly up to him, but wasn't strong enough. "I guess that doesn't work any-more," she admitted.

"What are you doing here?" North asked Jack.

"Same as you," Jack replied, and then he motioned to Jamie.

"Wow! It is you!" said Jamie. He looked at North and Tooth in awe. "I knew it wasn't a dream."

"Jack! He sees you!" North exclaimed.

"Wait, where's Bunny?" asked Jack.

North looked down at the ground. "Bunny wasn't so lucky," he said sadly.

"Oh no," said Jack as he noticed a regular-size bunny in the sleigh.

Jamie let out a giggle. "*That's* the Easter Bunny?"

Bunny was frustrated. "*Now* somebody sees me! Where were you about an hour ago, mate?"

"What happened to him?" asked Jamie. "He used to be so huge and cool, and now he's . . . cute."

Bunny was at the edge of his nerves. "Did you tell him to say that?" he asked Jack. "That's it! Let's go! Me and you! Come on!"

Jamie quickly tried to explain. "Actually, he told me you were real. Just when I started to think that maybe you weren't."

Bunny stopped hopping toward Jack. He

turned to Jamie. "He made you believe? In me?"

Jack grinned. "One down, four hundred million to go."

Bunny returned Jack's smile, but it didn't last very long. The group heard more thunder in the distance. Pitch was floating on nightmare sand in the air above them.

"Get Jamie out of here," Jack ordered.

"What are you going to do?" asked North.

"I have no idea," Jack admitted, and then, as the Guardians hurried away with Jamie, he jumped up and flew furiously fast at Pitch.

Pitch was shocked to see Jack flying up toward him after what he had done to him in Antarctica, but he sighed and flew down to meet him.

Jack and Pitch sailed right into each other and tumbled throughout the town. Snow and nightmare sand swirled everywhere as Pitch tried to obtain Jack's staff once again.

"You should've stayed out of this, Jack," Pitch warned. The two were now rising above the town. "If you had, it would be over by now. And you'd be no worse off."

"But everyone else would be," said Jack.

Pitch couldn't believe what he was hearing. "Since when do you care about everyone else?"

With a burst of energy, Jack pulled his staff free from Pitch's grip, but before he knew it, the nightmare sand had twisted around it and pulled it away from him.

Without his staff, Jack couldn't fly. Pitch started to wave good-bye as Jack fell to the ground.

Meanwhile, Pitch's Nightmares were searching everywhere for Jamie and the powerless Guardians. Bunny led the way into an alley, only to find that it was a dead end.

Thud! Jack was back, having fallen into a Dumpster.

Jamie and the Guardians helped Jack up to his feet. "That was a good try, Jack!" North said encouragingly. "*A* for effort!"

But Jack could only think of one thing. "My staff. It's gone."

More thunder cracked behind them, and a shadow began to creep along the walls of the alley.

Pitch's voice boomed down. "All this fuss over one little boy. And still he refuses to stop believing. Very well. There are other ways to snuff out a light."

As if to prove his point, Pitch's shadow began breaking the lights in the alley. Jamie looked scared.

"You want him, you're gonna have to go through me!" said Bunny.

Pitch laughed. "Look how fluffy you are! Would you like a scratch behind the ears?"

"Don't you even think about it," Bunny retorted as he jumped back up into the safety of North's arms.

Then Pitch's shadow disappeared and was replaced by the sound of hooves trotting down the alley's pavement. The real Pitch appeared, riding on Onyx. "I can't tell you how happy it makes me to see you all like this," he said. "You look awful."

It was true. Because of what Pitch had done, the Guardians were weaker than they'd ever been. And yet they still tried to protect Jamie.

"Jack, I'm scared," Jamie confessed in a small voice.

A memory stirred in Jack. He remembered his sister saying that when the ice began to crack all those centuries ago. Jack remembered how he had assured her that she was going to be all right.

Now Jack knew what to do. He faced Jamie. "We're gonna have a little fun instead."

Pitch continued to close in on them. "So what do you think, Jamie? Do you believe in the Boogeyma—"

Pow! A snowball hit Pitch in the face. Jamie giggled as Pitch wiped away the snow. Jack handed Jamie another snowball.

"I do believe in you," Jamie told Pitch. "I'm just not afraid of you."

Pow! Another snowball hit Pitch in the face. With Pitch distracted, the Guardians, Jack, and Jamie ran out of the alley, but not before Jack picked up a few supplies out of the trash . . . wooden crates, a trash can lid, and a wok.

"Ready for a little more fun?" Jack asked Jamie.

Whoosh! A blue streak flew past a man walking his dog on the quiet streets of Burgess. Just like he did a few days ago, Jack was creating a path of ice with Jamie by his side. But this time, the Guardians followed on the trail in sleds made out of the wooden crates Jack had found in the alley.

"Yeah! Come on!" Jack encouraged.

"Cool!" added Jamie.

"Who needs a staff when a child believes in you? It's like the first time the reindeer flew," North observed.

"Let's go get your friends!" Jack said to Jamie.

Cupcake was lying in bed, the covers pulled way up over her head, afraid of falling asleep and having another nightmare, when a snowball pounded into her window.

She lowered the covers and saw something she'd never seen before: It was snowing inside her room! For the first time in a while, Cupcake smiled.

A few houses down, Pippa was also amazed by the snow drifting down in her room. She went to the window when she heard a knock on the pane. She couldn't believe what she saw: Jamie Bennett floating outside her second-story bedroom window!

"Jamie, how are you doing that?" she asked.

"Jack Frost," Jamie answered. "Come on, we need your help!"

Jamie zoomed across the street, and that's when Pippa saw him. "Is that . . . ?"

"Jack Frost!" Pippa heard Monty cry from inside his snowy bedroom.

The same thing happened in Claude and Caleb's bedroom.

"Wow!" Claude exclaimed, watching the snowflakes fall from his ceiling.

Then Christmas presents fell at the foot of their beds.

"Merry Christmas!" North bellowed.

The twins rushed to their window and watched the Guardians speed past on their sleds.

"Happy Easter!" added Bunny.

"Don't forget to floss," Tooth put in.

Then, to the boys' surprise, Cupcake sped by in her own sled.

"Jamie was right all along! The Easter Bunny is real!" said Caleb as a group of kids ran to catch up with Cupcake.

"And the Tooth Fairy," added Pippa.

"And Santa!" said Monty.

"They're all real!" cried Claude.

A few minutes later, Pitch stood on a rooftop, watching Jack, the Guardians, and Jamie and his friends come to a stop on their homemade sleds.

As the group looked up at him, he churned his nightmare sand, covering the sky above the town in pitch-black darkness.

"You think a few children can help you?" Pitch chided the Guardians. "Against this?"

Pitch directed the nightmare sand to wind its way through the town. Everything it touched was destroyed. Then the nightmare sand made its way toward the group.

Jack noticed the fear in Jamie's face. "They're just bad dreams," he assured him.

"And we'll protect you," added Bunny as he, Jack, Tooth, and North moved in front of the children, blocking them from the nightmare sand.

"Aww, you'll protect them." Pitch sneered. "But who will protect you?"

Jamie looked around at his friends. They all

looked even more scared than he did. Jamie was determined not to let Pitch win.

"I will!" he volunteered, and stepped forward.

Jamie's friends all did the same. Soon, Jamie, Cupcake, Pippa, Monty, Claude, and Caleb were standing in front of the Guardians. The nightmare sand rushed toward them.

"They're just bad dreams!" Jamie reminded his friends.

The kids all put their hands out as the nightmare sand barreled into them. But instead of knocking them over and hurting the Guardians, the black sand transformed into golden dreamsand!

"Whoa . . . ," said Claude in absolute wonder.

Every strand of nightmare sand that the kids touched turned to dreamsand. Soon, the Nightmares were running every which way, trying to get away from the dreamsand.

"Jamie, what's going on?" asked Pippa.

Pitch was wondering the same thing. His plans were crumbling along with his Nightmares.

Soon dreamsand was making its way into the bedrooms of children all over the town. Dreams were becoming sweet again.

In Pitch's Lair, the Mini Fairies were gaining strength. Baby Tooth perked up. Her wings began to flutter.

And just like the Globe at the North Pole, the darkened Globe at the center of Pitch's Lair began to glow with lights again. More and more lights sparked to life as the Mini Fairies opened the tooth boxes. The memories within the boxes returned to the minds of children all over the world.

Sophie looked out her bedroom window. Dreamsand rushed past, as if traveling down a golden highway from the sky.

"Pretty!" she exclaimed as a strand of dreamsand turned into a glittering butterfly outside her window.

As dreamsand made it into the windows of more and more sleeping children, the globe in North's sleigh began to glow with more and more lights as children began to believe. Soon, North could feel his power rushing back. He pulled out his swords, ready to destroy some Nightmares.

At the same time, Tooth's wings began to flutter again. Jamie and his friends cheered as Tooth zoomed through the air.

Tiny Bunny was being chased by a Nightmare. He tried to run and hide, but the Nightmare caught him by the tail. Bunny was prepared for the worst when all of a sudden, he grew into his old size again.

"G'day, mate!" Bunny greeted the Nightmare just before he flung his boomerangs and sliced the Nightmare in half.

Pitch continued to send his Nightmares into the fight, but the Guardians were now at their full strength. North threw a snow globe onto the ground, and the yetis and the elves from the North Pole came rushing in to help.

"No way!" Caleb and Claude exclaimed at the same time.

Elves parachuted in, bailing out of toy ducks and planes.

Bunny opened a big rabbit hole in the ground

and then welcomed his Sentinel eggs. Some of Jamie's friends hitched a ride on top of them.

Jack scanned the scene and saw Pitch sitting on Onyx on a rooftop. Pitch disappeared down the roof, and Jack ran to find him, with the Guardians in tow.

On the roof, Jack moved out of the way before Pitch's nightmare sand could hit him.

"Ho, ho, ho!" cried Bunny as he tossed boomerangs at Pitch.

Meanwhile, on the wrong roof, North burst out of a rabbit hole with his swords at the ready. "Hyah!" he yelled into the empty air.

On the ground below, the kids continued to face the Nightmares, reaching out and touching them, causing them to turn into golden dreamsand butterflies.

North jumped to the right roof and then knocked Pitch off the back of Onyx. Pitch made a scythe from the loose nightmare sand, just as North rushed toward him.

Clang! Pitch's scythe met with North's sword. Soon the other Guardians had Pitch surrounded.

"I hate you, Frost," Pitch hissed, backing into

an alley with the Guardians following close behind. He split himself into many shadows to distract them, then doubled back behind Jack. He held an ax made of nightmare sand in his hand.

"Jack!" Bunny warned.

But before Pitch could strike, a golden whip made of dreamsand bound Pitch's hands together. The whip was being wielded by none other than Sandy. Dreamsand flooded toward Pitch, and he was thrown back by it.

The other Guardians were filled with joy by the return of their friend.

Sandy rose above the battle, shooting strands of golden dreamsand in every direction. Nightmares quickly disappeared, leaving behind only happy thoughts.

There was so much dreamsand floating around that Sandy turned some into a gigantic brontosaurus. Everyone cheered as Sandy created more creatures out of the dreamsand.

Jack started a snowball fight. He hit Jamie first. Jamie grabbed some snow of his own and pelted Claude.

"Oh yeah? Bring it on." Claude took out an elf.

North pulled Jack aside.

"Your center?" he asked.

"It took a while, but I figured it out," Jack said.

North grinned and tossed something to Jack. Jack caught it and knew instantly what it was: a nesting doll that looked just like Jack! Jack smiled at North. North winked. Then he lowered his eyes as he was hit by a snowball. North turned slowly to face Claude and Caleb. For an instant the boys looked scared, but then North laughed.

"You're all on the naughty list," he said. "Bunny, think fast!" North joined the fun by smacking Bunny in the face with snow.

In the sight of all this fun, Pitch was miserable. He rose into the sky and saw not one ounce of fear as dreamsand creatures roamed the streets, and snowballs whizzed through the air.

"You dare have fun in my presence?" he cried out to everyone. "I am the Boogeyman, and you will fear me!"

He swooped down toward Jamie and his friends, but instead of catching them, the kids ran right through him. They didn't believe in him anymore.

The Guardians approached the now-powerless

Pitch. He turned toward the forest outside of town and ran.

But Pitch couldn't outrun the Guardians. They met up with him at the Pond.

"Leaving the party so soon?" North asked as Pitch crashed into him.

"You didn't even say good-bye," Tooth pointed out and then tossed a coin to Pitch.

"A quarter?" Pitch asked.

Whack! When Pitch wasn't looking, Tooth punched him in the jaw. One of Pitch's teeth slid across the ice.

"That's for taking my fairies," said Tooth.

Pitch scowled. "You can't get rid of me!" Pitch looked down. He was standing in the center of the ice-covered Pond. "Not forever. There will always be fear."

"So what?" North retorted. "As long as one child believes, we will be here to fight fear!"

Pitch pointed at hundreds of Nightmares emerging from the woods. "Really? Then what are they doing here?"

"I don't know," North said. "But they can't be my Nightmares. I'm not afraid."

"Looks like it's *your* fear they smell," Jack said to Pitch.

Suddenly, high in the sky, the clouds parted and moonlight shone through. Pitch's eyes grew with terror as the Nightmares moved closer to *him*.

"AHHHHHH!" Pitch tried to run from the Nightmares, but a cloud of black sand swept him through the forest. Finally he was pulled under the old, broken bed and back down into the dark hole in the forest floor. The hole closed itself up, and Pitch was gone.

CHAPTER ELEVEN

The sun began to shine over the Pond. Jack found his staff lying on the ground. He lifted it toward the sky.

The moon was there, shining its last moon-beams before the sun's rays took hold of the day.

Jack looked up to see a faint smile on the barely visible face of the Man in the Moon. Jack smiled back.

Then he heard Tooth laugh. He looked around to see that he was surrounded by the Guardians.

"What's going on?" Jack asked.

"Are you ready now, Jack?" North asked. "To make it official?" A yeti handed North the ancient book of the Guardians. "Then it's time you take the Oath." North cleared his throat. "Will you, Jack Frost, vow to watch over the children of the world?"

Jamie and his friends—along with the other Guardians, yetis, elves, and eggs—made a circle around Jack.

"To guard with your life their hopes, their wishes, and their dreams? For they are all that we have, all that we are, and all that we will ever be." North finished reading the vow, and waited for Jack's answer.

Jack looked first at Jamie, then at North. "I will."

"Then congratulations, Jack Frost, for you are now and forevermore . . . a Guardian." North closed the book.

The kids cheered wildly. The yetis and the eggs celebrated.

"You're the man, Jack," said Claude.

Bunny congratulated Jack. "Good job, mate."

"Klassno!" North picked up Jack, giving him a hug with kisses on both cheeks.

Amid all the celebrating, Jack noticed the Mini Fairies flitting about, swooning and fainting with joy.

"Keep it together, girls," Tooth reminded them.

Caleb pointed to something huge in the sky. "Look!"

"It's Santa's sleigh," exclaimed Monty.

After everything they'd seen, the kids still couldn't believe their eyes at the sight of the sleigh.

"Everyone loves the sleigh," said North, chuckling. Then North saw the sun rising higher in the sky. "Time to go," he told the Guardians.

Sandy threw dreamsand up into the air. It floated down softly and landed on Jamie and his friends, who began to yawn and stretch.

Bunny gave Sophie an egg. She giggled as she ran back to her brother. "Happy Easter, ya little ankle biter. I'm gonna miss you," he called after her.

"You're leaving?" Jamie asked drowsily. "But what if Pitch comes back? What if we stop believing again? If I can't see you . . ."

Jack knelt down to look Jamie in the eye. "Hey, hey, slow down. Are you telling me you stop believing in the moon when the sun comes up?"

"No," Jamie replied.

"Okay, well, do you stop believing in the sun when the clouds block it out?"

"No," Jamie repeated.

"We'll always be there, Jamie. And now"—
he pointed to Jamie's heart—"we'll always be
here." Jack smiled. "Which kind of makes you a
Guardian too."

Jamie was proud.

"Let's go home. I'm sleepy," Claude said.

"I can't keep my eyes open," Pippa agreed.

"What time is it?" Caleb asked. "I'm dreaming."

Jack smiled as he stepped into the sleigh with
the other Guardians.

Jamie waved good-bye as the sleigh began to
speed along the ground. He ran behind the sleigh
until it lifted into the air, heading for the North
Pole.

Jack was happy. Happy to have helped defeat
Pitch and to finally know who he really was: a
Guardian. He turned back to watch Jamie as the
sleigh careened into the morning sky. He formed a
snowflake in his hands and let it go. . . .

THE END